I0764594

Dressed in Grey and Blue

Walter Duncan's Memoirs and History of Nashville During the Civil War

Don Cusic

Dressed in Grey and Blue
By Don Cusic

ISBN 978-0-9855561-2-9

Brackish Publishing
P.O. Box 120751
Nashville, TN 37212

Production Coordinator
Jim Sharp
Sharp Management

Interior layout and design
www.PricelessDigitalMedia.com

CHAPTER 1

Adelicia Acklen was a beautiful woman, a warm gracious lady who had the gift of enchantment. I was pleased and honored to be considered a friend of the Acklens, having gotten to know them and their family from my work as publisher and editor of the Nashville Lance and Shield newspaper.

Colonel and Mrs. Acklen came to Nashville each summer to escape the heat and humidity of Louisiana. Adelica Acklen had seven large cotton plantations in Louisiana that covered thousands of acres. In Nashville the couple built Belle Monte mansion, a beautiful, lavish home with an estate that contained an art gallery, gardens, an aviary, lake and a zoo. It looked like an Italian palace and, indeed, that's what it was built to look like. Adelicia Acklen was believed to be the richest woman in the United States, so she could well afford it.

The Acklens were hospitable people and often opened their estate to visitors and held parties at Belle Monte, better known as Belmont. The party they held in September, 1860 was a farewell to Nashville soiree because they were going to Louisiana to administer their Louisiana plantations and needed to oversee the harvesting and selling of their cotton crop.

Since it was an election year, there was much talk of politics and most of those at that party supported John Bell, a native son candidate. Not that everyone was for Mr. Bell, of course; there were many who favored John Breckenridge. The Democratic party was split in this election; in addition to Bell and Breckenridge, there was Stephen Douglas, but whether those on the lawn that day supported any of those three candidates, I can safely say that no one there—at least as far as I knew—supported the abolitionist candidate from Illinois, Abraham Lincoln, nor did they embrace the idea that the Republican Party should be running the United States. That was almost a side issue since Lincoln would not be on the ballot in Tennessee.

The day was gorgeous, all bright sun and clear blue sky, and, as I sipped my lemonade, I noticed Mrs. Ophelia Monahan, a recent widow whose husband, Floyd, had been a prominent banker in Nashville, and her daughter, Miss Rachel Monahan, a lively, feisty girl who attended the Nashville Female Academy. Rachel's father had died quite suddenly—a heart attack, I'd heard—while working in his office. That had been in June, about three months after my wife, Mary died.

Mary and I had been married for almost 28 years. My family came from Baltimore and we moved to several places before settling in Nashville in 1820. I was 20 when I married Mary and we had five children—three of whom survived—as I learned the printing trade and then became editor and publisher of a newspaper that did quite well. After Mary died I sold the newspaper for a nice sum, sold our home and, aided by the benefits of some fortunate investments, settled into a comfortable life of retirement with a room at the St. Cloud Hotel.

It is always awkward to speak to someone whose beloved has died and most are reluctant to do so; after all, what words can do justice to such a sorrow? But I knew, since I had recently been through that myself, that the person whose loved one has died appreciates any words of kindness and, in fact, feels less awkward than someone saying those words. And so I walked over to Mrs. Monahan and Rachel and said, "Good afternoon, ladies. It's good to see you here and I hope you're doing well, considering your recent loss."

"Oh, we're doing quite well," said Rachel. "This is such a lovely place and a lovely day and the people are so lovely as well."

Mrs. Monahan smiled and remarked, "My Rachel is quite talkative, Mr. Duncan. She loves the social world and talking with people. And I hope you're also doing well, sir?"

"Quite well," I answered. "Like Rachel said, it's a beautiful day and we're at a beautiful place. And I, too, enjoy the company of so many interesting people."

"Oh, these really are the best people in Nashville," said Mrs. Monahan. "Mrs. Acklen always makes it a point to have the most interesting guests at her home. She has such good taste in everything, especially when it comes to people."

Rachel noted that the Hardings and the Overtons were there and said, "The Hardings have been wonderful to us since Papa passed. We had dinner at Belle Meade just last week."

"I'm sure that was a delightful evening," I said.

"Is Mrs. Polk here?" asked Rachel.

"No, she doesn't really leave Polk Place except for church," I replied. "And if she were here it might be a bit awkward with all the John Bell supporters."

"Why would that be awkward, Mr. Duncan?" asked Rachel. "Doesn't she support a Democrat for President?"

"A Democrat, I'm sure," I replied. "But probably not Mr. Bell."

Rachel asked "Why?" and Mrs. Monahan reprimanded her, saying "Oh, Rachel, we shouldn't be discussing politics at such a beautiful party with all these friends around." I smiled at Mrs. Monahan and said, "You're right, of course, but Rachel sounds interested in the events that have shaped our city" and I told Rachel that Mrs. Polk's husband, the late President James K. Polk, clashed with Mr. Bell on a number of occasions. I told her that I believed that Mrs. Polk would prefer Mr. Breckenridge but she is a gracious lady, with diplomatic skills, so I'm sure she would be reluctant to reveal her preference for President in this election. Or at least she would never reveal that information to me or most of those here today. Still, I was certain there were some who were much closer to Mrs. Polk than I who would be told in no uncertain terms who she felt would make the best President during the 1860 election.

I then turned to Mrs. Monahan and said, "Isn't this a delightful gathering?" "Delightful, yes, delightful," she replied. "It certainly is. I only wish that my daughter was not so inquisitive and, shall we say, probing with her questions. And how have you been, Mr. Duncan? I know you've had a loss as well."

"I'm doing well, thank you," I said. I told her that I had sold my newspaper and moved into the St. Cloud Hotel and enjoyed my retirement from the business world. That's when Rachel said, "Oh, they have the best food at the St. Cloud. I hope we can join you there sometime."

Mrs. Monahan was a bit embarrassed when Rachel said that and eyed her daughter rather sternly before apologizing, "Rachel is quite forward. Please forgive her."

There was no need to forgive and I told Mrs. Monahan that "Rachel is feisty and full of life and that's a blessing. Those qualities always make for an interesting young lady and interesting conversations. I would love to have you two join me for dinner some time at the St. Cloud."

Mrs. Monahan thanked me and Rachel said she would remind her mother of that offer "from time to time." I could only smile at that remark. Rachel and Mrs. Monahan curtsied as I bid adieu and walked off to join in other conversations.

That September day is one I shall never forget because I have often looked back on it and wished that time had stood still on that day. Who was to know the election just two months away would be the beginning of a time of terrible turmoil in this country?

A week or so later I invited Mrs. Monahan and Rachel to dine with me at the St. Cloud but, at the last minute, Mrs. Monahan felt ill and so Rachel came alone. Mrs. Monahan was concerned about Rachel coming alone but I assured her I would look after her and make sure she returned home safely.

Rachel proved to be quite an interesting and lively dinner companion, full of questions, mostly about Mrs. Polk. Rachel was intrigued by Mrs. Polk, whom she had seen but never met, and so almost as soon as we were seated she asked, "Tell me about Mrs. Polk. What is she like?"

I told her that Mrs. Polk was the wife that every politician dreamed of having. She dedicated her life to helping her husband realize his political ambitions which, to be honest, were her ambitions as well. She liked the political world and she functioned well in it. There was no better political operative and advisor than Mrs. Polk and James Polk would never have become President without her.

Rachel was quite a talker and we covered a wide variety of subjects. She was a young lady who did not like a pause in the conversation; when one occurred, she quickly filled it. Some of it was girl interests—she talked about clothes that were fashionable, what other women wore and even what some men wore. She had definite ideas about clothes and liked to be fashionable and up to date.

We also talked about the upcoming election and Rachel seemed quite well-informed. Her mother liked John Bell but Rachel seemed to lean towards John Breckenridge, although neither could vote in the election. She asked questions about my late wife and our marriage and seemed informed on the news of the day.

It was no wonder that Rachel did not have a young man courting her; he would have to be quite sharp to keep up with her. He may have thought that some of her conversation—like local and national politics—were not proper subjects for a young woman to discuss, but I found her refreshing and enjoyable. I couldn't help but wish that some of the young men about town were as lively, interested and intelligent as she was. I also found myself thinking that if I were a younger man I might wish to court Rachel, but I was no longer a young man. However, I had three sons who were not married and imagined that she and Edward would make a handsome couple; their interests seemed to be compatible and they were nearly the same age.

CHAPTER 2

John Bell won the votes of Tennesseans in his quest for the Presidency; he carried the state by better than a two to one margin. The election was held on a Tuesday and the next morning it was certain that neither Bell nor Breckenridge, the other candidate favored by Southerners, would be President.

In the 1860 Presidential election, Bell carried Virginia and Kentucky in addition to Tennessee but Abraham Lincoln won that election, a fact that upset most Nashvillians who were, on the whole, advocates of keeping the Union together. The idea of secession was heavy in the air after the election—there were rumblings from neighboring states—but the idea was not embraced by most Tennesseans. Most Nashvillians felt the secessionists were too hot-headed and their own views towards preserving slavery and the Southern way of life were more reasonable and could be accomplished by staying in the Union.

Tennesseans in Nashville were, for the most part, fearful of abolitionists and believed that slaves were well cared for. Slave owners felt their slaves looked to them as protectors. Besides, the slave owners reasoned that the relationship between slaves and owners was in accordance with the Laws of Nature. The fanaticism stirred up by the Republican Party was fighting against a higher order, according to the slave owners, when abolitionists sought to free the slaves. The owners argued that it wasn't just a political issue, it was

Biblical, and many of the city's ministers and religious leaders backed them on that view.

Some Negroes were already free and lived in Nashville. This rankled some whites but in February, a bill to expel free blacks from the state was defeated in the state legislature. There was, of course, an underlying and continuous fear, ever since the Nat Turner incident in Virginia, that blacks would rise up in rebellion. However, planters who owned slaves believed that Negroes were better off under the care of a good, kind master. That's why it always baffled whites when a slave tried to escape from his master. A little over a month after Abraham Lincoln was inaugurated President, a local newspaper reported that a slave named "Alex" was discovered in a large box which had been shipped from Nashville to a Cincinnati mercantile firm with "Express Negro" printed on the outside. The slave was discovered when the box broke open.

It has now been thirty years since that War started and when I look back it seems so obvious that we were headed towards War and those planters who owned large numbers of slaves were only fooling themselves when they believed that slavery was best for the Negroes. A man tends to see things from his own personal perspective and justifies whatever he does as best for all concerned when, really, it is what is best for him.

We tend to believe that others see things as we do so we're always surprised when someone disagrees with us on our basic beliefs and assumptions. We always believe that what motivates us is what motivates others, that our own views emanate from a true line of reason and those who don't see things as we do are misguided, mistaken, misled and that if only they would listen carefully to what we have to say then pure reason would wash over and cleanse the error of their ways.

We say we know that isn't really true and yet, deep down, we believe it. We tend to see ourselves as the sun in our own solar system and everything revolves around us when, in fact, we are really a small moon, circling a planet that is circling a sun. I must admit that before the slaves were free I often wondered how they could make it on their own, but people are enterprising and find a way. We underestimated Negroes, forgot they were humans who often showed remarkable abilities and skills when they worked in homes and on plantations. We were fools, really, us white folks for underestimating a people who could be incredibly resourceful. What held them back—and what still holds them back—is not their blackness but the white folks who have figured out how to get power and keep it and perpetuate their positions through generations.

CHAPTER 3

My oldest and youngest children were daughters; Elizabeth, our oldest, died when she was six from a childhood disease and our youngest, Sally, only lived four months. She was a weak, sickly child from the time she was born and her health never improved. My oldest son, Robert, had a small farm to the south of Nashville. He had dark hair, like his mother, and a dark complexion. John Overton had leased a small farm to Robert with the agreement that Overton would receive a fourth of the income from the farm and, at the end of five years, Robert would own it. He had married but his wife died in childbirth; two days later, their young son also died. I did not see Robert often; it had been a year since the deaths of his wife and child but he preferred to stay on his farm most of the time and seldom came into town.

My second son, Edward, worked for the Nashville Banner newspaper as a reporter. When I sold my paper, Edward, who had worked for me, quickly obtained a job with the Banner; he was a good reporter and wrote well. Edward had sandy hair and an outgoing personality; he made acquaintances easily and was easy to converse with.

My youngest son, Matthew, worked in the telegraph office as a telegrapher; he learned Morse Code from an old friend of mine who worked for Western Union. Matthew was quiet and moody but was a reliable worker. He had done well in the telegraph office and had the confidence of his superiors. Matthew had the ability to please those he worked for and always stood in good stead with his employers.

Edward and I often talked about politics and the news floating about. Edward talked regularly with political and business leaders and was quite perceptive when it came to judging character. Matthew also kept abreast of the news because of the telegrams flowing in and out of that office. Both Edward and Matthew were always intrigued with Mrs. Polk, a very public figure who always remained a mystery of sorts.

Our family was always close but after Mary died my sons and I did not see each other as much. A mother is always the glue that keeps a family together; children always come home to a mother. After I sold our house and moved into the St. Cloud Hotel, it was not the same; where I lived was no longer "home" and so the boys and I met in restaurants or in the lobby but it was never like sitting around the fireplace at home and just chatting. I didn't realize what I had lost when I sold our home, although it would have been difficult to keep up a house with my wife gone.

There was something else that compelled me to move and that was the memory of Mary, which permeated our home. After she died there I felt I needed to leave that house. It was just too difficult to live there with the loneliness. Everything reminded me of her and I knew that, even though I had loved her, I needed to move on and not allow her death to hold my final years hostage to her memory. And so I sold that house and moved.

CHAPTER 4

Mrs. Polk was the Grand Dame of Nashville. As the widow of a former President she deserved honor and respect and, as a formidable woman whose presence demanded honor and respect, she received all of that as she lived to perpetuate the legacy of her late husband.

Mrs. Polk was quite serious minded and could be rather cold and aloof. She certainly had self-confidence—she never lacked for that—and was handsome. I first met her when her husband was in the Tennessee legislature during the early 1820s. She was always pleasant but I knew she looked at me as someone who, as editor and publisher of a newspaper, could help further her husband's ambition and she treated me accordingly.

Mr. Polk was not a man who impressed you with his charm or knowledge. He had no wit, to speak of, and was not graceful in his language or actions. You'd expect a politician who rose to be President to be a great orator but Mr. Polk did not fit that mold. He could not quote from literature or engage in a debate with elegance or any of the attributes you expect from a great man. Mr. Polk was a workhorse who worked doggedly day after day until his efforts were rewarded.

For her part, Mrs. Polk kept up with the issues of the day. She knew about power, who had it, who wielded it, how to work it to advantage and, ultimately, how to obtain it. She could not make her husband President by herself; Andrew Jackson was the star of the Democratic party and James Polk hitched his wagon to that star.

There are many men who aspire to a life in politics but few manage to win an election and then persevere through future pitfalls, disputes and challenges, both personal and professional. It's hard to say what makes a successful politician, if success is defined by a lifetime spent in political office. It's not always the best man or the smartest or most competent man who makes politics his life but it is always someone with money, or access to money, who can draw support from influential and powerful people.

I have known a number of politicians in my life, talked with them at length and in depth and I can safely say that there are many fools in the profession. On other hand, I have also met those who were caring men who read deeply and formed enlightened views on the issues of the day. Unfortunately, those men were few and far between and those who tended to dominate the political world were those who had the ability to smile, shake hands, kiss babies and possessed an incredible amount of luck.

It's hard to over-emphasize luck in the political life; some have it and some don't and there seems to be no rhyme or reason why some are so blessed while others aren't. Timing is also important, being in the right place at the right time with the right skills for the moment. Ah, the moment—that's the essential problem with politicians, whose decisions are usually based on their re-election so the closer they are to that election the more likely they are to make foolish, short sighted appeals to the lowest of the common masses. The world has to live for a long time with short term expedience.

When Andrew Jackson left Washington at the end of his second term as President, he returned to Tennessee and the Polks traveled with him on his way to the Hermitage. Polk was re-elected for another term to the House of Representatives but as Speaker he had to deal with two old enemies, John Bell and John Quincy Adams, on a daily basis. That led Polk to run for Governor of Tennessee and he won that election.

Mr. Polk, with Mrs. Polk behind him, had political aspirations higher than Governor and before the 1840 election wrote a letter to President Martin Van Buren, who was running for re-election, and asked to be considered as a candidate for Vice President. That was Polk's ultimate political ambition: to be Vice President of the United States.

Van Buren lost that election and Polk lost his bid for re-election as Governor. Polk ran for governor again in 1843 but lost that election as well which, by an odd set of circumstances, led to his election as President, an unlikely victory if there ever was one.

Martin Van Buren, Jackson's vice president, sought the Presidential nomination but Texas was a major issue; Andrew Jackson wanted it annexed to the United States but Van Buren and Henry Clay opposed the annexation. Van Buren thought he could win the nomination without Jackson's support but Jackson still had a large, strong following in the Democratic party and the annexation of Texas was a popular issue. Jackson sent word to Polk, requesting a meeting at the Hermitage. Polk came, they talked and, after Polk agreed that Texas should be annexed, Jackson let it be known that he supported Polk as the Democratic nominee for President.

So Polk, whose highest political ambition was to become Vice President of the United States, found himself as the nominee for President. At their home in Columbia, Mrs. Polk coordinated the work on his campaign. Working as a team, they wrote numerous letters, kept the newspapers informed of his stand on issues, and courted campaign workers and party leaders.

James Polk was a frail man and would never have withstood the long days and nights of a campaign for the Presidency without his wife who, politically astute and knowledgeable about the issues, drove the campaign forward with her boundless ambition. Polk defeated Henry Clay during that campaign, although he failed to carry his home state of Tennessee. For most of those in Tennessee, James Polk was a man who had lost the last two gubernatorial elections, the longest of long shots for the Presidency, but Mrs. Polk never doubted this dark horse could win.

CHAPTER 5

The Friday evening after the Presidential election I took Mrs. Monahan and Rachel to the theatre and bought seats in the Dress Circle, which cost me 50 cents apiece. The Southern Star Company put on an excellent evening's entertainment with the Zouaves from Europe. The group performed some military maneuvers and pantomimes and brought to life the battles in the Crimea.

During the evening I remarked to Mrs. Monahan and Rachel about the performers and we talked about theatre in general. Mrs. Monahan was a widow who was smothered in sorrow, still grieving for her husband and, although I grieved for my departed wife, I would not stop living and being of the world now that she was gone. I received the impression that Mrs. Monahan remained cloaked in grief and could never really enjoy herself at the theatre—or anywhere else—without her husband.

Not that her husband was a devotee to the theatre; she remarked, more than once, how he disliked the theatre with its noise and rabble. Mr. Monahan enjoyed an evening with cultured gentlemen, discussing the politics of the day while sharing some bourbon. Mrs. Monahan and the ladies always adjourned to another room and spent the evening in talk, often about other ladies who were not there.

Rachel, on the other hand, was fascinated by the theatre. She saw it as a great adventure and felt she had travelled to another country when she watched the Zouaves. To Rachel, life was a great adventure, meant to be tasted and touched and theatre was a vehicle that transported her outside daily life into exotic lands with foreign people. She was a young lady full of enthusiasms who plunged headlong into any new experience, relishing it and then savoring the memory.

During that evening I found myself talking with Rachel much more than Mrs. Monahan as the show progressed. It was a crowded house and I don't believe there was a single empty seat. Mrs. Monahan remarked several times that it was unpleasant and stifling to be in a hall with so many people and so many of those people unknown to her, possibly dangerous and threatening, and not in the circles where she normally socialized. After Mrs. Monahan remarked that she was uncomfortable, I almost suggested we leave; if I had only been with Mrs. Monahan I would have left but Rachel was energetic in her love for the show and the large crowd seemed to energize her. If Mrs. Monahan was uncomfortable then, well, I thought, she'll just have to tolerate it because I could not bear to pull Rachel away from this packed theatre and the Zouaves. Besides, I knew that if I did, Rachel would protest vehemently. Since I also enjoyed the theatre a great deal—it was one of my favorite forms of entertainment—I decided that Mrs. Monahan would just have to sit there for a few hours because, I had long ago decided, it is not right for one person to spoil the enjoyment of others.

I have always made it a point to enjoy myself wherever I am and whatever I am doing. It is wonderful to meet new people, to see and hear new things and to welcome in new experiences. I see no reason to be miserable when a simple change in outlook will create a joyful experience.

CHAPTER 6

My family moved to Nashville in 1820, shortly after I turned eight. I apprenticed for a newspaper printer before I started my own newspaper. The paper had done well and I sold it in January, 1860. Mary was sick at the time—she died in March—and I needed to spend time with her. It was difficult to watch her die; she was sick for a year and a half and during that time I watched her succumb to a sickness the doctors were helpless to cure.

We had a good marriage and I was thankful my early life was filled with the happiness and joy that Mary brought me. We were different, quite different; she disliked socializing with politicians and other prominent people so I often went to events alone. Part of the reason was because she had children to raise and she devoted herself to our children. After our children were grown, Mary preferred to stay home or socialize with her group of friends and we each allowed the other the freedom to do that. We did, of course, spend evenings together at the theatre and she loved musical concerts but, for the most part, she preferred a quiet evening at home rather than the hustle bustle of a newspaperman's life, whose evenings were often spent in the company of men who drank heavily, smoked cigars and talked politics and current events. Even if Mary had wanted to be part of that life, women were not allowed to join those conversations. During the evenings when we went to a dinner at someone's home, the men adjourned to a room to converse while the women spent time in another room. Mary did not enjoy those evenings so I often went alone to those private dinners.

Since 1860 was an election year, I knew I could get a good price for the newspaper because there would be plenty of subscribers and advertisers during an election year. I was also concerned about what life would be like without Mary. Even though I often went out alone in the evenings, she was my anchor, the one who kept me balanced and at the end of an evening I was always glad to come home to her. I enjoyed evenings with her quiet companionship and wondered what I would do when I found myself no longer married and had to fill the empty hours alone.

I was correct in the assumption that the Lance and Herald would bring a good price during an election year and so, shortly after turning 48 years old, I sold the paper and retired from the newspaper business.

As a newspaper man, I was used to gathering facts and I can tell you that in 1860, according to the census conducted that year, there were about 30,000 people living in and around Nashville; about 24,000 were white, there were 5,000 black slaves and 1,000 free blacks. Out of the approximately 17,000 who lived inside the Nashville city limits, there were around 13,000 who were white, almost 4,000 black slaves, over 700 free blacks and over 200 prostitutes. It was the second largest city in the South, behind New Orleans.

Nashville was a transportation hub; there were five railroads that came into the city, which was a major center for the distribution of goods. The rail connections led to Decatur, Alabama, Louisville, Chattanooga and Atlanta. The Cumberland River was deep enough for steamboats and barges most of the year. There were a number of manufacturers, grocery companies, wholesalers of dry goods and hardware and eleven banks. Nashville was a progressive city and during the twenty years between 1840 and 1860 the population more than doubled.

Nashville itself was divided with the wealthy mansions isolated in one section while middle class and poor citizens had their areas. There was a fairly large professional class of lawyers, judges, professors, bankers and, yes, newspaper publishers. In the poor districts the majority of the Irish immigrants lived in mostly disgusting conditions. On the riverfront was the "Jungle" or "Smokey Row" comprised of bars and brothels. That was a dangerous area and those who ventured there had better be aware of the whores, thieves and pickpockets who would swindle them out of their money. It was an area known for its violence and a man of character and integrity could not feel safe there. The women who inhabited that area were not suitable for respected mothers, sisters and wives to encounter.

The largest religious group in Nashville was the Methodists, although the Baptists were not far behind in numbers. The white churches had free blacks as members but there were separate services for each. There were also several black congregations.

The largest plantation, Belle Meade, had 3,500 acres and was owned by William G. Harding. It was located to the west of the city and known for breeding fine racing horses.

There were, of course, both rich and poor in Nashville, although they never mixed socially. The Southern Way of Life dictated that manual labor was for slaves and poor whites. Those in a higher social class worked with their minds; they gave orders, they did not take them. They tended to give orders to slaves who took care of the mundane day to day activities that take up so much time in life while their masters focused on lofty ideals and thought-producing leisure.

The importation of slaves had been banned by the state of Tennessee until 1855; however, after this time, Tennessee was a primary location for slave trading. The slaves were brought into Nashville by steamboat, railroad and wagon and bought and sold at auctions. Many believed there was nothing wrong with this; indeed, many thought it was the best way to monitor the slave trade because if it were not out in the open, then slave trading would be done in an underground economy and that was not best for either slaves or owners. There was no quality control and weak or sickly slaves could be pawned off on unsuspecting masters. Also, the masters recognized that when their actions were in the public they were more likely to act nobly. This, it was generally accepted by city leaders, was good for both slave and master.

The free blacks in Nashville caused a problem with the white citizenry. First, it set a bad example for slaves, who might try and become free themselves. The deeply held belief that slavery was good for blacks—a belief instilled and endorsed by the great majority of the white population—was challenged when free blacks were allowed to live in the city in open view. Blacks could own property—could even own slaves themselves—but they could not vote or testify against whites in Court. They were required to carry their "Freedom Papers" wherever they went and present them to any white who challenged them. Most whites did not want free blacks living in Nashville but they were tolerated and, for the most part, did not cause any great problems.

CHAPTER 7

Edward and I spent several evenings during October talking about the political climate in Nashville. The topic that consumed most of our conversations was the issue of secession and whether or not states had the freedom to secede.

There had been talk amongst southern states about secession from the Union for a number of years. Many believed the Constitution of the United States allowed this and embraced the idea of a state freely choosing to either stay in or secede from the Union. The question of slavery kept coming up and many Southerners felt that those who did not live in the South did not understand the necessity of slavery nor the fundamental Laws of Nature that were the foundation for the Southern Way of Life. Those abolitionists sought to abolish slavery, ignorant of the economic disaster that would result or the impossibility of blacks living with whites as equals.

There were concerns that blacks would be unable to take care of themselves without white masters, that the Negroid race was child-like and incapable of fending for itself and without the care, guidance and protection of whites, their world would collapse. It was widely believed that blacks were innocent creatures who should not be subjected to the harsh cruelties of a world where they had no protection.

Amongst loyal white Southerners, there was never a belief that whites and blacks could mix socially, nor should they try. There was concern for the women and daughters of white families who might perhaps be subjected to the animal passions of a black male. The thought of a violent black male with an innocent white woman made a Southerner's blood boil. On the other hand, there was concern that some white women were weak and could not control their passions and, in this condition, would be defenseless against a black male who would take advantage of her. Mostly it was a matter of money and economics. The white planters, who were the economic backbone of society, could not survive without slave labor and the economy of the South could not thrive if there were no slaves. The abolitionists simply did not take this into account.

Edward and I discussed these ideas and issues time and again. We saw the abolitionist's point but always concluded that the South as we knew it could not exist without slavery; it was simply unimaginable. We were not immune to the argument of the slave's humanity but there was no political solution that would solve or even address that because when politics and economics meet, money always speaks louder. And you can't tell a rich man to give up his money or power because he will never hear you.

CHAPTER 8

When the Constitution was discussed in the South, the discussion was whether it was a compact or a contract. Many, perhaps most of those I conversed with in Nashville, agreed it was a contract. Still, those Tennesseans wanted to honor that contract and stay in the Union; other states did not want to remain and there were fire breathers itching for a confrontation.

After the election in November, the South Carolina legislature called for a special convention; the fire breathers kept pushing for a showdown and every day they'd pour a little more fuel on that fire. Those fire breathers were outside the political system but they worked night and day to sow as much discord within the system as they could. They were not accountable to the people or to the body politic and they held no office with responsibility. They were men who tried to tear down institutions; they were not builders. They were men who clamored for power but promised only ruin if it were given to them. They built bonfires of dissent and incited hot emotions but they could not govern and, indeed, had such a disdain for the skills that governing requires—such as letting your opposition be heard, representing a wide variety of viewpoints, getting a consensus by giving up some of what you want—that they would be a disaster if ever put in a position of governing. Still, their voices drowned out the voices of reason and moderation so politicians had to listen and provide some kind of answer or else lose votes. You can't ever expect a politician to do something that will cause him to lose votes.

The Governors were a little more cautious; they were all waiting for somebody else to make a move, so they were waiting on each other.

One issue pushing them forward was the sale of the cotton crop. If the South could get their cotton overseas to England and Europe for sale, then they'd have money in their pockets and be in a position to bargain for a Treaty that would establish the South as a new, independent nation.

On February 4—a month before Lincoln's Inauguration in Washington—a convention was held in Montgomery, Alabama to discuss forming a new nation. It was cold that day, close to freezing, when representatives from the states of South Carolina, Alabama, Florida, Louisiana, Georgia and Mississippi gathered. The North Carolina delegation arrived later.

This was the cream of the crop of politicians, movers and shakers in the South. It was an impressive bunch; 33 of them were lawyers and most had college degrees—some from Harvard, Yale and Princeton. A number of them had served—or were serving—in the United States Senate and House, in the Cabinet, or in state legislatures. Only eight did not own slaves.

These men were not united in their views; a good number did not want secession when they arrived. However, all of them wanted to get along socially when they gathered; this was, after all, the aristocracy of Southern society and even if their political views towards secession did not unite them, their Southern culture was a unifying force much larger than any political disagreement that might arise.

The convention was a secret meeting; there were no reporters or uninvited members of the public allowed. The men felt they could air their views more freely—and change their minds and their votes—if the public and reporters were not allowed. They also feared holding an election on secession at home; the assembled group felt they knew best and would make the correct decision if left alone to debate amongst themselves.

Ironically, one of the first things they did was pass a resolution banning African slave trade. This was not an anti-slavery platform but an economic one: the convention members felt the four million slaves in the South was enough to provide adequate slave labor for the future. The slaves would breed and so their population would increase. The Southerners would not have to depend on Northern merchants for slaves and the value of their slaves would increase if outside slaves were not allowed to enter into the current slave population.

Having lived through the administration of the inept James Buchanan as President, the Southerners agreed that two thirds of Congress should be allowed to remove a president and vice president from office—impeachment should not be required—if he could not perform his duties. This, they felt, would solve the problem of having someone as unfit for the office as Buchanan serving out his term.

Although there were no reporters allowed to attend the meetings in Montgomery, Edward went down and talked with those attending the convention during the evening hours. There were secrets to be kept but the men talked freely; they felt they were at the vanguard of something of immense impact and were proud to be part of those deciding the fate of the nation. These were men of power and they had large and powerful egos. They felt they were important and what they were doing was important and it is hard for anyone who carries strong convictions about the future of the nation not to broadcast those views to all who might listen. Part of being powerful is having others believe you are powerful and these men sought the respect of others in their group.

The group met to discuss the new government and the delegates from Georgia made it clear the capital should be in Atlanta and that a Georgian should be President.

Three days before the Convention, United States Senator Jefferson Davis returned to his home in Mississippi from Washington. Davis was a West Point graduate and fought in the Mexican War under General Zachary Taylor, who later became President. Davis married Taylor's daughter, although the General disapproved, but their marriage only lasted three months because she contracted malaria and died.

Davis had an impressive political background. He had served in the House of Representatives, as Governor and Senator of Mississippi, and as Secretary of War under President Franklin Pierce. He was a major political player on the national stage and opposed secession; however, he resigned from the Senate when he learned that Mississippi had seceded from the Union.

Jefferson Davis was only one of several who were considered for the Presidency of the new nation but when the Convention decided on Davis they handed the future of the Confederacy to a man who spent much of his time in indecision, always busy but not always doing business. Davis would study a subject intensely, fill his mind with facts and information, and bombard an opponent in debate with all this information to win an argument, but he was not a man with an imagination. Once he arrived at a conclusion, he clung to it, unable to admit there might be other solutions. He was a closed minded man whose obstinacy and pride forced him to cling to a conclusion and distrusted men who changed their minds.

I knew Jefferson Davis, had met him several times to interview him for the newspaper and found him to be a courtly man, full of courtesies and the ways of a Southern gentleman. I always felt he worked well in a group but did not see him as a solitary leader and wondered how a new nation would fare under his leadership. He needed to be a George Washington for the Confederacy and I did not find the character, decisiveness or leadership skills of a Washington in him.

Davis was a self-righteous man, fussy about trivialities and adamant that everyone act with formalities when dealing with him. He was a proud man, over-protective of his dignity who could never explain himself or his decisions; those around him were expected to never question his decisions but rather accept his certainty. If you disagreed with Davis, you didn't just come to a different conclusion, you were wrong. He was not a man who compromised.

CHAPTER 9

After Abraham Lincoln was elected President—but before he was inaugurated— seven Southern states chose to leave the union and form a Confederacy. This separate nation planned to settle the slavery question once and for all. There would be no states trying to abolish slavery nor would there be the problem in Washington of a "balance of power" where there were more non-slave states than slave states and therefore slave states would be under the thumb of Northern politicians bent on crushing the power of Southern states. That would be an impossible situation to live under and led South Carolina to be the first to secede. Their legislature voted on that before Christmas. In January, Mississippi, Florida, Alabama, Georgia, and Louisiana followed; Texas seceded on February 1.

Governor Isham Harris of Tennessee wanted secession in early 1861, but a February plebiscite to secede was defeated by Tennessee voters, who chose to remain in the Union. Then, on April 12, Federal forces invaded and bombarded Southern forces at Fort Sumter, South Carolina, which ended Tennessee's hopes for remaining in the United States. The fight at Fort Sumter led President Lincoln to issue a call for 75,000 troops but the Governors of Tennessee, Virginia, North Carolina, Missouri and Arkansas—none of whom were in the Confederacy at that time—refused. Almost overnight the hearts and minds of most Nashvillians changed from wanting to remain in the Union to wanting to join the Confederacy.

Less than a week after the attack on Fort Sumter, Virginia seceded, followed by Arkansas and then, on May 7, Tennessee formed an "alliance" with the Confederacy. On June 8, a state referendum on secession was voted on by Tennesseans; those in the middle of the state overwhelmingly voted to secede from the Union. This vote united the people of Nashville in opposition to the Union, although there were still strong Unionists in Nashville and East Tennessee was a stronghold of Union men. By this time, North Carolina had also seceded while Missouri declared neutrality. There were hopes that Kentucky and Maryland would join but their Governors held the reins on the public will and they remained in the Union. This meant there were eleven states who were part of the Confederate States of America, a new nation formed like the Union had been formed, by states freely choosing to be part of a country whose ideals, beliefs and policies they endorsed.

A state and nation needs an army and military units were formed in every county in Middle Tennessee. Some factories had begun to manufacture arms and supplies for the Confederacy. Still, most Nashvillians were reluctant to sense any danger from a Union army. Confederate military leaders did sense the importance of Nashville to the Union and sent a military engineer to the city to oversee the construction of fortifications but there were objections from citizens and few laborers could be recruited to build those fortifications. Instead, Nashvillians felt comfortable their city would not be touched by an invading army.

It is human nature, I suppose, to not want to face a problem until it is staring you in the face and it is difficult to convince either politicians or the public to solve a potential problem looming on the horizon. A problem has to be a visible threat before it is acknowledged. Until that time, there is an underlying belief with most people that a potential problem will never materialize, that it will be solved or diverted or solve itself or something will happen to cause it to disappear, or at least be a minor irritant rather than a massive problem too big to be solved quickly or easily.

The citizens of Nashville did not sense any danger from a Federal army and did not feel threatened by the gathering clouds of war. There was a general feeling that problems are meant to be solved when they become problems and, in their minds, a Federal army less than 100 miles away was not a problem and so they did not prepare as if there was a threat but rather like people who did not believe a war would ever touch their daily lives. They did not like being told what to do and so they ignored the pleas of a government whose job it was to protect their safety and preserve their freedom.

Nashville was expected to play an important role in the new Confederate nation. It was widely known as a center for medicine by the 1860s; it was the second largest, next to Philadelphia, for health care, which made it the leading city in the Confederacy for medicine. In downtown Nashville, the Maxwell House Hotel, a grand structure, was under construction, financed by John Overton.

The Confederacy established its first capital in Montgomery, Alabama but in the middle of 1861 the Confederacy moved its capital to Richmond, Virginia, where President Jefferson Davis presided. There were some who thought that Richmond was too close to Washington but Southern politicians felt that when disagreements were all settled—and many thought that would happen in due time—it would be advantageous to have the capitals of the two nations close to each other.

CHAPTER 10

Matthew came by my room late one Sunday night with news that came over the telegraph of a battle outside Washington; he delivered that news to our Governor and others. Matthew also sent telegrams, dictated by Governor Harris and others, to Jefferson Davis and other Southern leaders. The country seemed anxious for war.

There were two nations sitting side by side, each with an army, and when you have two armies marching around they're bound to run into each other and fight. That's just what they did. The first time was a Sunday in Virginia. The Battle of Bull Run was witnessed by a large crowd from Washington who came to Manassas to enjoy a picnic and afternoon battle. Wars are fun when you're a spectator unless the fighting gets out of its assigned field and into the spectators. It's also fun when there's no bullets, cannonballs, slashing swords, charging horses or blood running out of arms and legs but all of those things happen in a war and they happened that Sunday. This was a wake-up call for those who thought this War would be some kind of Grand Adventure.

The hopes of the Union army, which thought it would annihilate the Confederates in short order, were dashed when Southerners won the day. The crowd of picnickers scattered and went running back to Washington. At this battle, General Jackson acquired the nickname "Stonewall," supposedly because his brigade held strong against Union forces, which led General Robert E. Lee to remark during the battle that Jackson was "standing like a stone wall." Whether that was a compliment or a source of frustration because Jackson wouldn't move and attack is still contested amongst those who discuss Lee and Jackson.

Ten days later the Provisional Army of Tennessee became the Confederate Army of Tennessee and began training at a camp on the Nashville Fairgrounds. In August the Confederate government appointed commissioners to Britain and France in order to secure material and supplies from Europeans to aid their War effort. The South felt it was in a strong bargaining position because Europe needed cotton for manufacturing. As a matter of fact, the Confederacy thought they could control England and France with their cotton, withholding it or parsing it out to their advantage. It didn't work that way and England and France sat on the sidelines, waiting developments on the battlefield.

CHAPTER 11

In September, Edward brought me news that Ulysses S. Grant was appointed to command Union forces stationed north of Tennessee at the mouths of the Tennessee and Cumberland Rivers. General Albert Sydney Johnston assumed command of Confederate forces in Tennessee and Kentucky and spread his troops from Columbia, Kentucky through Bowling Green—about 60 miles north of Nashville—to the Cumberland Gap creating "The Line of the Cumberland." Residents of Nashville felt safe with General Johnston's troops stationed just to the north of them. Inside the city of Nashville, neither the Governor nor the Mayor was able to convince citizens to pick up a shovel or grab a hammer and build fortifications. The general feeling was that no foreign army would dare come to Nashville so we'd just carry on life as usual.

General Leonidas Polk, a relative of former President James K. Polk and Bishop in the Episcopal Church until he resigned, led Confederate troops into Kentucky and captured Columbus, bringing the War into that state and ending Kentucky's desire to remain neutral.

After Polk's troops captured Columbus, Grant captured Paducah, Kentucky with little resistance. This town was strategically located for future river campaigns leading into Nashville and Grant always smelled an advantage on the battlefield. The Confederates strengthened their "Line of the Cumberland." The troops were itching to fight and there were minor skirmishes near the Cumberland River in Kentucky where soldiers from both sides died.

General Grant had troops in Cairo, Illinois while Confederate General Felix Zollincoffer was confronted by an uprising of pro-Union mountain men in eastern Kentucky. It looked like the War was going to be a bunch of cat fights.

During those early days of the War, a number of politicians and former politicians managed to acquire leadership roles in the military because political connections were major determinants for those who sought to become members of the officer corps. General Zollincoffer was one of those. He had owned newspapers in Knoxville and Huntsville, had served in the army briefly in the Seminole War during the 1830s and held state office in Tennessee before he was elected to Congress for three terms.

I knew Felix Zollincoffer and knew that he did not want Tennessee to secede from the Union; he had gone to Washington as a delegate to a Peace Conference and expressed his desire that Tennessee remain in the Union. However, when Tennessee seceded, Zollincoffer volunteered to serve in Tennessee's army and Governor Harris appointed him Brigadier General.

CHAPTER 12

In January, 1862, the Confederates held two key forts on the Tennessee and Cumberland Rivers, Forts Henry and Donelson. General Lloyd Tilghman was named commander of those forts, which were key to stopping a back door invasion into Tennessee and Nashville by the Union army.

In Nashville, citizens and officials were in a near-panic over rumors that Northerners and Southern traitors would infiltrate the city and burn it. Citizens wanted loyalty checks to uncover subversives. Nashvillians didn't feel as safe as they used to, but they still didn't believe a foreign army could get to them. When you're in a war, you can't avoid a fight, but that's what a lot of the Union Generals did when that War started so Southerners felt a little safer.

Between Matthew's work in the telegraph office and Edward's reporting, I was kept abreast of all that was happening. I also read the newspapers regularly, including those which came in from out of state. The news coming into the telegraph office concerned me and I wondered about the fate of Nashville in the coming year. Edward shared those concerns but when I talked to local business leaders they seemed to brush off those concerns, convinced the city would remain unharmed.

On Monday, January 13, Major George H. Thomas led his troops to Mill Springs in Eastern Kentucky, which was held by Confederate forces under the command of General Zollincoffer. The Rebel troops were nearly out of provisions, surviving on half or one third rations. At Mill Springs Confederate troops found supplies and provisions and decided to take the offensive and attack Thomas's forces. At dawn, after marching since midnight, Rebel forces encountered Union Regiments. During this skirmish, General Zollincoffer was killed, the first General to fall in the Civil War. Since this was a Gentleman's War—officers on both sides often knew each other, had gone to school together and sometimes even roomed together—Union officers honored a fallen officer and had the Union surgeon embalm Zollincoffer and sent the body to Nashville, where he was buried in the City Cemetery.

If the Union army captured Forts Henry and Donelson, the Tennessee River led straight through the heart of the Western Confederacy while the Cumberland River flowed right into Nashville, where absolutely nothing had been done to prepare for an attack. The staff of General Albert Sidney Johnston thought an attack on Nashville was laughable—out of the question—because the city would be defended by Confederate troops in Bowling Green, about 60 miles north of the city. The Union army didn't see things that way.

CHAPTER 13

When General Grant's troops attacked Fort Henry, General Tilghman, who was in charge of the Fort, sent his soldiers to Fort Donelson. Fortunately for the Confederates, there had been a heavy rain storm during the night so Union troops were unable to cut them off. That was fortunate for the Rebels unless they liked being soaking wet and covered with mud.

As the walls of Fort Henry began to collapse from the shelling, General Tilghman lowered the flag and surrendered himself and the men inside. The surrender opened up the Tennessee River, and left Nashville and the western Confederacy vulnerable. General Grant led his troops toward Fort Donelson, which was located on a bluff above the Cumberland River.

Grant's troops attacked Fort Donelson but were repulsed by the Rebs. As the sun set, a freezing rain fell, a northern wind blew and the temperature dropped to 20 below zero. By the next morning, the land was covered with snow and trees were covered in ice. General Johnston hightailed it with his troops while inside the Fort General Floyd faced the problem of how to get his troops out of the Fort and march them 70 miles to Nashville.

That night the Confederate Generals planned a breakout at dawn from Fort Donelson; however, another winter storm hit and that morning there was ice hanging on bushes and trees. The two sides fought and after three hours there were numerous blood stains on the white snow but the road to Nashville was open. However, Rebel Generals in the Fort became indecisive and stayed in place, arguing about their next move, which allowed Grant to move his forces forward.

Trapped in the Fort, the Confederate Generals agreed to surrender except for Colonel Nathan Bedford Forrest, who left with his cavalry saying that he'd come there to fight, not give up. Confederate General Buckner, who lent Ulysses Grant money back when the latter was broke and needed money to get home, thought he would obtain good terms for his surrender when he sent soldiers under a white flag to deliver that message to Grant. Meanwhile, General Pillow and Colonel Forrest, accompanied by both cavalry and infantry troops, crossed an icy river with no resistance and headed towards Nashville.

General Buckner was the first Confederate General to surrender during the Civil War; since he had attended West Point with a number of officers from the Union army—a band of brothers—he expected a gentlemanly response and was no doubt shocked when General Grant replied to his letter that "No terms except an unconditional and immediate surrender can be accepted. I propose to move immediately upon your works." That gave General U.S. Grant his name—the U.S. now stood for "Unconditional Surrender"—and at least one Rebel general learned that a Gentleman's War had its limits and old friendships didn't count for much when two armies had guns pointed at each other.

Buckner reluctantly accepted Grant's terms. The soldiers departing with Pillow, Floyd and Forrest left him woefully short of troops to put up a decent fight, which meant that Grant captured over 12,000 prisoners, which were sent, along with General Buckner, to prison camps in the North.

CHAPTER 14

On the morning of February 13 the Nashville newspapers reported that a Union boat had fired on Fort Donelson but the boat had been repulsed. The report was reassuring to Nashvillians until later that morning when a telegram reported that Federals had attacked the Fort. The Confederates remained optimistic at the end of the day because reports indicated the Rebels had whipped the Feds.

On February 14, Nashvillians received news that the Federals had captured provisions and several trains at Bowling Green and that town was being evacuated as it burned. This news, as well as the information that Union troops had cut off escape routes from Rebel soldiers in Bowling Green, spread rapidly and left the population disheartened. General Johnston let it be known that he would not send any troops to help those at Fort Donelson and the people in Nashville openly wondered what would happen to them and their city if Northern troops entered.

On February 15 the ice and snow covered a freezing Nashville. City officials, concerned about the Union army entering Nashville, removed from the Commissary and Ordnance Departments items they did not want to fall into Union hands. However, there was still optimism in Nashville as news arrived that the Confederate troops would prevail at Fort Donelson and then, at 1 p.m., citizens were informed the Rebels had whipped the Union army.

Good news continued to flow into Nashville about the Fort Donelson fight with reports generally positive. A number of citizens outside Nashville were in the city to hear more news of the battle at Fort Donelson. The newspapers printed "Extra" editions and Southerners extolled the superior virtues of their Rebel soldiers. Dispatches from Fort Donelson were read aloud to citizens during the day and Nashvillians felt sure that Southern troops would win.

On Saturday night most Nashvillians, confident that Confederate soldiers would be victorious, went to bed comfortable and secure in the belief they would be safe in the coming days.

CHAPTER 15

There was a buzz swirling through Nashville on Sunday morning, February 16, that Fort Donelson had surrendered, the Confederate army was taken prisoner, that General Buell and 35,000 Union soldiers were in Springfield, about 25 miles north of Nashville and Union gunboats had passed Clarksville and would be in Nashville around three that afternoon. There was unfathomable disbelief the Rebel army could have been defeated. Rumors ran rampant throughout the crowd, which increasingly became fearful and panic-stricken.

The rumors created a whirlwind that swirled like a vicious tornado throughout the city as fears intensified until people were frantic with nervous activity and gossip. Fear is a madness that seizes the brain and strangles reason. Nashville was swallowed by this madness as people voiced conjectures and musings became facts with legs that galloped through gatherings of people and ignited even more fears. Panic has no brake once it starts rolling through a crowd caught in the grip of unreasoned fear.

There were crowds outside the Tennessee Capitol where Governor Isham Harris's office received a message from General Johnston that Fort Donelson had fallen. Some officials insisted that Governor Harris issue a proclamation and state the facts in a manner to calm the frantic crowd but Harris refused to issue any proclamation. He was not alone; neither General Johnston, Mayor Cheatham, or the editors of the newspapers issued any fact-based reports. The crowds, meanwhile, were seized by fear that Union soldiers would invade and destroy their city.

Preachers did nothing to calm the crowds that Sunday morning as the panic increased. Late that morning Governor Harris notified the population that women and children should be evacuated by two that afternoon because Union troops would shell the city. This multiplied the horrible panic, which continued to spread like a fire with a strong wind. Men, women, children—old and young—ran in all directions, grabbed valuables and loaded them on wagons or headed to the railroad depot to flee the city. Huge sums were charged by those who hired out horses, wagons and carriages so that only the wealthy could afford them; others fled the city on foot, carrying with them all they could manage.

Governor Harris was advised by General Johnston to evacuate the State's archives, which were packed and shipped to Memphis on a special train that afternoon. Harris and other heads of government accompanied those archives to Memphis. The legislature convened quickly and issued a notice they were gathering in Memphis to conduct state business. At this time it was learned a resolution had been adopted during a secret session of the legislature a few days before to remove the seat of government from Nashville as a temporary measure. Meanwhile, the legislators, in obvious fear, fled to the rail depot carrying whatever possessions they could haul.

When it became obvious that government officials were fleeing the city, panic multiplied further and spread faster. When General Johnston's army marched through the city without stopping, residents knew that Confederate forces would not halt a Union advance and they would be at the mercy of Northern barbarians who would not hesitate to murder, rape and plunder.

No one knew what to do; should they flee immediately or stay and take their chances with the Union army? Many had no choice; they had to stay. The trains were packed beyond capacity—many rode on the tops of cars—and there was no horse to be found who could haul a wagon or carriage. People abandoned their homes to strangers and left valuables with only the faintest hope they would be safe.

The biggest fear was of fire. If the Union army set the city ablaze and then shelled it, those left would be trapped and the city would be a mass of blackened and charred remains. No city officials or leaders—military or otherwise—did anything to mitigate the fears or control the panic, which paralyzed the thoughts and actions of the citizens of Nashville. There was no voice of reason, no statement of assurance that there was any hope or solution for impending doom. Hospitals flew yellow flags and bankers packed up their money, notes and valuables and fled, leaving the city with empty bank buildings.

Each of my sons came by the St. Cloud Hotel and urged me to leave, but I couldn't. This was my home and I really had nowhere else to go, although I'm sure I could have gone to Atlanta or Montgomery or some other Southern city and made a life for myself. But Nashville was my city and, although she was in danger of destruction, I knew I had to stand with her. If she fell, then I would fall too; I was firm in my convictions.

CHAPTER 16

General Johnston was in Edgefield, the residential part of the city, across the Cumberland River and east of the Courthouse, Capitol and business district. He met with Mayor Cheatham and informed him the Confederate army would not fight to defend Nashville. Mayor Cheatham returned from his meeting with the General and told the populace that he would lead a committee of citizens with a flag of truce to formally surrender the city when the Union army arrived. He told citizens that provisions from the commissary would be distributed equally and he would negotiate with Union officers to protect the rights and property of citizens. These assurances calmed the fears of a few people.

When the clock struck three, neither the Union army nor its gunboats had arrived. The crowds were somewhat calmed by the knowledge that time remained before their arrival; however, fear and panic erupted when rumors spread that gunboats would arrive around midnight. A regiment of troops were detailed to guard the city that night as many spent sleepless hours.

A heavy rain fell on Sunday night and continued to fall on Monday morning as Generals Floyd and Pillow arrived. Fear and hope alternated amongst citizens who heard that Colonel Forrest was coming to Nashville and Confederate President Jefferson Davis had ordered that Nashville be held at all costs. The mud filled streets were crowded with citizens and Rebel soldiers in wet and muddy clothes.

Confederate soldiers wandered the streets with citizens; everyone was tired, hungry and rain-soaked. Although there were no Federal troops in sight, Confederate soldiers continued to move South until there were few left by nightfall.

Reliable news was scarce; the post office had been moved to Murfreesboro two weeks before so no mail had arrived in Nashville for two weeks. The Nashville newspapers suspended publication and businesses were all closed, leaving employees with nothing to do but wander the streets and spread gossip and rumors.

There was no calm in the city, although rampant fear and panic had subsided a bit as people talked amongst themselves on the streets in front of closed businesses. Almost every conversation was speculation of what would happen next and what each should do. The wealthy had, for the most part, left and the remaining soldiers entertained those gathered around them with their exploits in this great adventure.

Thousands of poor residents remained in Nashville because they had no way of leaving the city. The military took over the railroads and those renting horses and carriages would only rent the few remaining at a cost that equaled the purchase of the horse and carriage.

General Pillow finally spoke to a crowd assembled on the Public Square at seven on Monday evening. In his five minute talk he told his audience the Confederate army would not defend the city; instead, city officials would surrender the city to the Union army. The General sought to assure the crowd the Federals would only be in Nashville a short while and then the Rebel army would return to drive them back across the Ohio River. He also told the crowd that

Union officers would behave as gentlemen before he left for his home near Columbia, about 30 miles south of Nashville.

General Floyd also spoke to the crowd, telling them the Confederates would defeat the Feds as soon as they lured them away from their gunboats and back into the mountains.

That night two Confederate gunboats were burned at the wharf in Nashville and another worrying rumor circulated that the Texas Rangers, serving under General Johnston, had announced they would rather see Nashville burned to ashes than be in Union hands. Now the citizens of Nashville feared not only Union troops but Confederate troops as well who both—according to a number of citizens—were ready to put the torch to Nashville.

CHAPTER 17

A cold, soaking rain poured down on Tuesday morning and the city was a sea of mud. There was a near riot at the depot where goods were distributed because citizens hauled off items with complete disregard to order, rules or regulations. Four shopkeepers were shot when they turned back a mob of citizens. It was a scene best described as mob hysteria by the time Colonel Nathan Bedford Forrest rode into the city with his cavalry. Forrest and his troops charged the crowd and brought order to the scene and allowed wagons to be loaded with provisions so they could be shipped south to Rebel soldiers.

The bridge that crossed the Cumberland River, linking Edgefield with the business district, was supposed to be burned on Monday night but on Tuesday morning it was still standing. Citizens were unruly to the point that there was fear a riot would erupt as goods from government warehouses continued to be distributed. A number of citizens wanted the suspension bridge across the river saved because it was the key passage that connected the two sides of the river but the military insisted it be burned.

Wednesday brought another rash of thunderstorms and heavy rains. Colonel Forrest remained busy in the downpour moving supplies from warehouses to the train. A prayer service that evening at Second Presbyterian Church attracted a larger than usual crowd, fairly evenly divided between Union and Confederate sympathizers. As the congregation stood, a member offered a prayer "to bless and prosper the Southern people," which caused about half the congregants to sit, then another prayer was offered "for the prosperity of the Union and the blessing of the Union army," which caused the first half to sit down and not participate. The group was reconciled when a prayer was proposed "to commit their differences to the infinite wisdom of God."

At ten that evening, the suspension bridge was torched and cables were cut, sending it into the Cumberland River. The Rebel army had gathered all the firearms they could find so there were few left in Nashville for citizens to defend the city.

Train cars were packed to capacity but V.K. Stevenson, president of the Nashville and Chattanooga Railroad, ordered a special train for him and his family, which left Nashville that night. John Bell, former Congressman and Senator and defeated presidential candidate of the Constitutional Union Party in the 1860 election left for Rutherford County and then Huntsville, Alabama; his wife, a member of the local Confederate Nurses Association stated before fleeing, "had my husband been elected this War would never have taken place." Also fleeing the city were pastors of the First Presbyterian Church, Tulip Street Methodist Church, Hobson Chapel Methodist Church and the editors of the Nashville Christian Advocate and the Tennessee Baptist's publication along with some prominent planters who had plantations further south. A number of doctors and surgeons left town, leaving several thousand patients in Nashville hospitals.

Someone who refused to flee was Mrs. Sarah Polk, who declined her family's advice. At her home she kept holdings of the Tennessee Historical Society and boxes of jewelry, diamonds and silver from Mrs. Adelicia Acklen.

I stayed as well. I was not a young man and had lived a good life and I believed that things are never quite as bad as they seem and, since this was my home, why run away?

CHAPTER 18

On Saturday, February 22, heavy sheets of rain fell most of the day and there was flooding in and around the city to the point that trains were unable to travel. General Grant, at his headquarters in Fort Donelson, declared that Tennessee west of the Appalachian Mountains was under martial law.

It was a week spent in waiting. The Federal army did not arrive that week, although some Federal spies came into the city. The Rebel army was packing and sending supplies from the warehouse, stopping Nashville citizens from getting to those supplies. Citizens were angry and upset, which caused Forrest's cavalry to charge the crowd on Wednesday, swords drawn and loaded pistols cocked. On Friday, Mayor Cheatham ordered the fire department to spray the crowd with fire hoses in an effort to restore order.

It seemed like a miscarriage of justice as law abiding citizens received no supplies while hucksters, con men and merchants held an abundance of supplies. Rain, which was heavy on Monday and Wednesday, came again on Saturday. There was flooding in the area as creeks rose and overflowed.

Rumors swirled as citizens speculated or passed on what they heard to other citizens or even strangers. The rumor receiving the most attention was that since General Johnston did not feel Nashville was worth defending then General Buell did not feel it was worth taking. It was both a relief and an insult.

Sunday morning, February 23, was beautiful; the air was warm and the sun shone brightly. There was water in the streets—some up to the second story of houses close to the river—and an abundance of mud in the rest of the city which caused people and horses to slip and slide. But at least the sun was out.

Federal soldiers came to Edgefield sometime around nine that morning. Word that Federal pickets were in the city spread quickly and citizens stood on the west side of the Cumberland River and looked across. The steamboat that ferried citizens back and forth across the river was stopped and Union soldiers sent word they would like to meet with Mayor Cheatham, who was ferried across the river in a small boat.

The meeting with the soldiers was brief and when Mayor Cheatham returned to the Public Square he informed citizens he had met with the Captain of an Ohio Calvary. There were murmurs throughout the crowd; a mere Captain? Why wasn't a General there to meet him? The message the Captain delivered was good news for Nashville citizens: he wanted the Mayor to assure citizens that the property and rights of Nashvillians would be protected.

That afternoon, the Mayor again was ferried across the river and met with a Colonel from an Ohio cavalry and returned to the Public Square to again assure citizens their property and rights would be protected. Some of that "property" was Negro slaves and Mayor Cheatham asked the Colonel directly "What about the Negro question?" The Colonel replied that "property of every citizen, of whatever description" would be protected. At the Public Square, the Mayor conveyed these assurances to Nashvillians, who were comforted they would not lose their slaves. The Mayor then urged citizens to continue on with their daily life as if these were normal times and that a General would arrive shortly to take military possession of the city.

In the middle of the day, Confederate Cavalry Captain John Hunt Morgan, with a guerilla band of soldiers, led his men to the river and managed to sink a steamboat the Federals had used to ferry troops across the river. Morgan sent three men to board the steamboat, had the crew leave and then set fire to the boat; however, the steamer was chained to the wharf and the chains could not be broken so she could not float downstream and spread her fire to other boats. With this deed done, Morgan and his men fled east towards Lebanon.

Meanwhile, Colonel Forrest, in command of the military in Nashville, spent that day organizing his retreat from the city. Helped by prominent citizens like plantation owner William G. Harding and Mayor Cheatham, Forrest commandeered horses, mules and wagons and ordered both citizens and slaves into service as he packed wagons of ammunition and loaded them on the Tennessee and Alabama Railroad, burned and spiked the remaining guns and set fire to what was left in the arsenal before he left the city at nightfall for Murfreesboro.

The crowd was somber, silently watching from sidewalks. Newspapermen with the Union army reported that a few Negroes rejoiced but the overall mood of the crowd was sadness and a feeling of humiliation their city was now under the control of the Union army.

CHAPTER 19

Early on Monday morning a fleet of steamboats carrying Union troops approached Nashville on the Cumberland River. That evening Union Generals Buell and Mitchell arrived in Edgefield and Buell notified the Mayor he would like to meet with him and a committee of citizens the next morning.

On Tuesday, more boats carrying soldiers and supplies arrived at the river landing and a number of citizens gathered to watch. The flotilla included a Federal gunboat that tied to the wharf and pointed all of its guns at the city. Each Federal soldier had 40 rounds of ammunition but citizens were calm and resigned to their fate. The Ohio regiment had a band who came ashore and played a series of songs, including the "Star Spangled Banner" and "Yankee Doodle" as they marched to the Public Square, then to the Capitol where Union General Nelson, in the name of the United States, took formal military possession of the capital of Tennessee.

William Driver was a Nashville resident and a Unionist. He was a former ship captain from Salem, Massachusetts who reportedly received a flag for his birthday and named it "Old Glory." In 1837 Driver quit the sea and settled in Nashville because he had relatives living here. Driver proudly flew "Old Glory" from the front of his home on patriotic occasions but as War clouds gathered he was afraid that Old Glory would be confiscated by Confederates. Driver hid the flag by sewing it inside a bed comforter; however, on Tuesday, February 25 Driver was at the State Capitol with "Old Glory," which was hoisted.

When General Buell met a committee of citizens led by Mayor Cheatham, the citizens requested that Buell issue a proclamation outlining the policy of the Federal government but the General declined and insisted his actions would speak for themselves. Meanwhile, Federal troops entered Nashville after disembarking from transport ships. Regimental bands played as soldiers marched to the Public Square; when they played "Dixie," which surprised some of those gathered, there were enthusiastic cheers and shouts from the crowd. By late afternoon there were around 12,000 Union troops in Nashville, most of them camped in the Southern part of the city.

On Wednesday a proclamation was issued by Mayor Cheatham that assured citizens they and their property were safe and that business should be conducted as usual, although the proclamation prohibited the sale of liquor.

CHAPTER 20

On Thursday, February 27, General Grant came to Nashville and, along with his staff, paid a courtesy call on Mrs. Polk at Polk Place.

The Polks acquired their home, originally known as Grundy Place when it was the home of Judge Felix Grundy, for their retirement after his Presidency ended. Grundy was a long-time friend of the Polks. Before the inauguration of Zachary Taylor, the Polks left Washington. When they arrived in Nashville the Polks were welcomed by an enthusiastic crowd, which escorted them to the courthouse square where Governor Neill Brown and President Polk spoke and then greeted a number of citizens who came to meet him. The home was not quite finished so they stayed at a hotel, then visited friends and relatives in the area before they moved into Polk Place.

President Polk aged a great deal during his Presidency. In Nashville, he spent his time at Polk Place arranging his papers but did not live long enough to fully enjoy his retirement. On Sunday, June 3 he became ill with symptoms that indicated cholera; he survived a few days, improving a little before he died on the afternoon of June 15—about six weeks after he moved into his home. He was 53 years old. His tomb was at Polk Place.

General Grant and his fellow officers arrived at Polk Place, which had a tall, wrought-iron fence surrounding it and was guarded by imposing gates. There were four large columns on a portico and the main entry from the portico was a large doorway that opened to a hallway, which opened on the left and right into large parlors.

According to a correspondent with the New York Times, who was with Grant that day, Mrs. Polk greeted the group "with polished coldness. She was simply polite and ladylike; in no case patriotic. She hoped that the tomb of her husband would protect her household from insult and her property from pillage; further than this, she expected nothing from the United States and desired nothing."

Mrs. Polk was imposing and could be cold and aloof, even amongst people she knew and liked. It was no surprise that she treated Grant in such a manner. After visiting Mrs. Polk, General Grant returned to Fort Donelson.

On the evening that Grant left town, I was in my room with Edward when we heard a knock on the door and opened it to see Rachel Monahan. "May I enter?" she said. I, of course, let her in although it was not proper for a young lady to enter a gentleman's room alone, but it was also not proper for an invading army to take over your city so we accepted liberties in our behavior.

Rachel said her mother was scared to death in their home and worried sick about what would happen to them. They were not without means but had nowhere to go; Mr. Monahan's lone relative, an elderly brother, lived in Atlanta, which was a possibility, but Mrs. Monahan's closest relatives lived in upstate New York.

We spoke briefly before I suggested to Rachel that we should go to the dining room and sit at a table to talk. Edward and I had not had dinner and, although she at first said she was not hungry and tried to beg off dinner with us, soon acquiesced and ate heartily.

Rachel was angry, upset and concerned, but she was not afraid. She was disgusted with the Nashville politicians and business leaders—the upstanding citizens of the town—who fled and left the rest of us to fend for ourselves. She saw them as cowardly, disloyal, frightened beings who showed their true colors when a real crisis occurred. Those were not the kind of people who engendered admiration in Rachel; she was a fighter and looked for those who would fight. I cautioned her that true bravery would not come from fighting the Federal soldiers head on—you were certain to lose that fight—but to undermine them in subtle ways and trick them into relaxing their guard, defeating them with stealth rather than physical power and strength—which we did not have.

Rachel told me that some of her friends had husbands and fiances who had joined the Southern army and she wanted to help, somehow, and would try to find a Southern soldier who could claim her respect. She said that with a forlorn look in her eyes, as if she had waited too late to find a young gentleman and now, would be without a way to help the Rebels fight the Union invaders in this War of Northern Aggression.

Edward was quiet during the meal but I could sense his feelings that he, too, needed to do something. I had mixed feelings about that. On one hand, Edward was a grown man, able to choose whatever path he wanted to follow but, like any father, I was concerned that one of my sons would be in a battle and there was no way to predict the outcome of either the battle or my son.

I wondered about Rachel and Edward and thought they would make a fine couple. They were both bright and energetic young people with a native intelligence and a fire that burned within. I could not help but think of them together in the future but, with the future being so uncertain and the time being such a difficult time, it was hard to even imagine a future, much less a quiet, peaceful one where a young couple could enjoy a long lasting happiness.

CHAPTER 21

At the end of February, citizens could read daily newspapers again; the Banner, which had suspended publication, resumed and a new newspaper, The Nashville Times, published by employees of the Union and American, began publication. A rumor circulated at the end of February that Rebel forces had re-formed in Murfreesboro and planned to re-take Nashville; that rumor proved to be false.

Union commanders and soldiers who thought that Nashville citizens would welcome them and rejoice at being liberated were in for a shock. Instead of being happy that Union troops had arrived to protect them, the good citizens of Nashville felt they had been invaded by a foreign army and were under the thumb of an occupying force. That image of joy and relief the boys in blue expected to see was a mirage. Although there were a number of Union sympathizers in Nashville, citizens' feelings toward the Union occupiers tended to be one of hatred of unwelcome invaders.

The people of Nashville, I always found, are a friendly, welcoming people who open their hearts and homes to strangers. But it is different when someone comes into your home uninvited after pushing in the door; no one wants their home violated and that's what it feels like when someone enters uninvited and unwelcome. Those Union soldiers thought they were doing us a great favor by coming into our city and our homes to protect us against a War with the Confederate army. Well, even if there was a grain of truth in that sentiment, the people of Nashville would rather have been left to their own fate than have an outside fate thrust upon them.

On the first of March, General Buell set up temporary headquarters at the St. Cloud Hotel and paid his respects to Mrs. Polk; he was accompanied by 28 officers. Mrs. Polk received them politely and they remained at Polk Place for about an hour.

Two days later General Buell established his headquarters at 13 North High Street, about two blocks north of the Capitol. The vacated home of V.K. Stephenson, a short distance away, became the headquarters for other Federal army commanders.

We learned that President Lincoln had appointed Senator Andrew Johnson to be Military Governor of Tennessee. Johnson, from Greenville in East Tennessee, had served two terms as Governor of Tennessee from 1853 to 1857. When the United States Senate confirmed him they also awarded him the rank of Brigadier General in the Federal army.

CHAPTER 22

Matthew alerted me he'd received information in the telegraph office that Andrew Johnson left Washington by train, accompanied by his son, Robert and several others, and travelled to Cincinnati. From there he went to Louisville by boat then boarded another train for Nashville.

Late in the evening of March 12, Andrew Johnson arrived in Nashville in a foul mood and went straight to his room at the St. Cloud Hotel. The next evening, he made his first public appearance. After a concert by the army band in front of the hotel, Johnson spoke for an hour from the balcony. I stood below the balcony and heard Johnson state that the "cause of the War against the Union was not slavery but 'disappointed ambition' and that treason must be crushed and traitors punished."

Parson Brownlow, an East Tennessee Unionist, arrived in Nashville and told Union troops that "the Rebel masses should be bloodied with grape shot and their leaders hanged. Give grapes to the masses and hemp to the leaders." Brownlow was the kind of man you never wanted to see in authority; he was a firebrand and fervent loyalist who viewed everyone who disagreed with him as an enemy. Men like that stoke the fires of emotion but are not fit for the day-to-day steadiness and even temper that is required of someone in the position of authority.

Johnson felt there was reason to fear Nashvillians; a number were in command positions with the Confederate army. Six days after he arrived, an "Appeal to the People of Tennessee" was distributed to Nashville citizens. The broadside stated Johnson's mandate "to preserve the public property of the State, to give the protection of law actively enforced to her citizens, and as speedily as may be possible to restore her government to the same condition as before the existing rebellion." He encouraged citizens to unite with him in this effort and believed there was an undemonstrated support for the Union in the hearts of most of the citizens of Nashville.

That same day two newspapers, The Times and The Patriot, stopped publication after their editors met with Johnson and concluded they would rather give up their publications than continue under Johnson's dictates.

Johnson could not tolerate anyone who questioned his decisions; further, he was plagued with poor judgment. From his years as Governor, Johnson had developed an intense dislike for Nashville's leaders and prominent citizens. One of his first acts was to require that political leaders in Nashville take an Oath of Allegiance to the United States; if any refused, they were removed from office and replaced with Union sympathizers, then arrested and charged with treason. This meant that anyone who questioned his decisions was guilty of treason.

This order was issued on March 25 and required Oaths be signed and returned within three days. The day before the deadline the City Council voted to return the Oaths unsigned because, they stated, the Oath only applied to officials of counties and states, not municipalities.

The day after the deadline Johnson ordered the arrest of Mayor Cheatham. Other city officials were also arrested, including aldermen and councilmen, because they had not signed the Oath. Johnson named replacements who signed the Oath.

On Sunday, March 30, Thomas and Joseph Brennan were arrested because their foundry had manufactured cannons for the Rebels; the next day James Hamilton and Thomas Sharp, whose manufacturing firm stopped making plows to manufacture cavalry sabers for the Confederate army, were arrested.

Also arrested were George W. Barrow, who was one of the Tennessee representatives who negotiated Tennessee joining the Confederacy and William G. Harding, who was head of former Governor Harris' military and financial board; an arrest warrant was issued for John Overton, owner of Traveller's Rest and considered the richest man in Tennessee.

Most Nashvillians sided with the Rebels but there was a core group of Unionists in the city as well who supported the occupation and Governor Johnson. Although they were much fewer in number, the Unionists were vocal in their allegiance and supported Governor Johnson's edicts.

CHAPTER 23

The citizens of Nashville learned of the Battle of Shiloh on Wednesday, April 9 and were stunned with disbelief; not only were they shocked that the Confederate army was defeated, they were shocked at the number of men lost and that Rebels would not be coming to Nashville to re-capture the city. After that battle, twelve hospitals were set up by the Federals to take care of wounded soldiers.

The hospitals in Nashville—which included churches and other buildings that had been converted—had 14,000 men after the Battle of Shiloh; 60 to 100 died each day. Among those wounded at Shiloh was Mrs. Polk's nephew, Confederate Captain Marshall T. Polk. Mrs. Polk received permission to bring her nephew into her home and nurse him back to health; Captain Polk lost a leg but soon re-joined the Confederate army on crutches.

The Confederates were concerned the east-west railroad from Memphis through Corinth, Mississippi to Chattanooga, and then branching off with one branch running through Atlanta to Charleston and Savannah and the other north through Knoxville to Lynchburg and Richmond, was in danger of being captured by the Federals. This railroad was critical, the backbone of the Confederacy, which led to a decision from Richmond to amass an army in Corinth to defend it.

During March, Confederate forces were building in Corinth, about 125 miles southeast of Nashville. General P.G.T. Beauregard was head of the Army of the Mississippi; Generals Braxton Bragg,

Daniel Ruggles, Leonidas Polk and Albert Sidney Johnston were with him.

Most of the Rebel army was "green," they had no experience in combat or even being soldiers, and General Beauregard failed to take into account problems with terrain and undisciplined troops. Beauregard planned a surprise attack against Union forces on April 3 but plans fell behind due to a disorganized march out of Corinth. Heavy, cold rains fell for several days before they left Corinth, which made travel on the muddy roads nearly impossible as wagons and artillery were constantly bogged down as the Rebels headed north out of Corinth into Tennessee. Those problems were compounded by a shortage of gunpowder, food, medicine and other essentials because of the Federal's capture of Nashville.

The plan was changed to attack on April 4 but that, too, proved impossible as the largest Confederate army ever assembled proved to be an unwieldy mass. At a Council of War the Confederate commanders debated whether to return to Corinth or push forward; the consensus was made to continue north but the final decision was made when Federal troops on reconnaissance ran into some Confederate troops and a skirmish ensued. Rebel forces kept moving forward and totally surprised Union commanders, who thought the Rebels were still in Corinth.

That Sunday a bright sunshine filled the skies as the biggest American battle ever fought began in Shiloh, Tennessee, about 100 miles southwest of Nashville.

The Confederate troops fought well and claimed victory at the end of the day; General Beauregard sent a telegram to Nashville that evening claiming "complete victory," although the commander of that battle, General Albert Sidney Johnson, was killed when a musket ball severed an artery in his leg while he sat on a horse observing the battle.

The next day, Grant received reinforcements; further, his reinforcements meant he had fresh troops while the Rebels were exhausted from the previous day's battle and had to contend with Union gunboats firing shells every 15 minutes during the night. Rebel reinforcements failed to appear so the Rebs were cold, tired and wet after trying to rest during an all night rain that turned to sleet in a cold wind.

General Grant struck the Confederate army at dawn the next day; shortly after four in the afternoon General Beauregard ordered a retreat to Corinth. The only Rebel hero that day was Colonel Nathan Bedford Forrest who ordered a charge from his cavalry against a force that outnumbered him five to one. Forrest led the charge only to discover the rest of his troops did not follow; he found himself in the midst of a sea of blue and while slashing and hacking had an enemy muzzle stuck into his ribs and discharged; it lifted him off his saddle but he managed to stay on his horse. The bullet lodged beside his spine but, undeterred, Forrest continued to fight his way out of the mass of blue coats and grabbed a Union soldier by his collar, swung him onto the back of his horse and used him as a shield as he raced away. Once out of range, Forrest threw the soldier on the ground and rode on to join his men.

About 100,000 men fought at Shiloh; 24,000 were killed, wounded or captured. Union losses totaled 13,000 while Rebel losses were 11,000, which meant that about one in four who fought at Shiloh was either killed, wounded or captured during that battle, more than had been lost in all three of the previous Wars of the nation combined: the Revolutionary War, the War of 1812 and the Mexican War.

In Nashville, the Union army needed to make the city a fortress so they conscripted whites, free Negros and slaves to work on forts in and around the city. The Fort on St. Cloud Hill was built like a star with ten points and then a wooden stockade atop it. There were blockhouses at the Fort, which allowed the army to have a good view south of Nashville. If a military force approached from the South, those in the fort were bound to see them.

CHAPTER 24

Governor Andrew Johnson was escorted from the St. Cloud Hotel to his office at the Capitol after an assassination attempt in early April. Johnson was not a likeable man, although he got along with young women well enough. He was harsh in his policies; in early April he arrested five preachers who would not sign the Loyalty Oath as well as a Judge in Sumner County.

The Union sympathizers in Nashville and they remained nervous about the general population, which primarily sympathized with the Rebels. The Unionists feared that citizens loyal to the South would join together one night and massacre all who sided with the Union. Word spread amongst the Unionists the slaughter would occur on the night of April 12 and the signal to start the slaughter would be a ringing church bell, but all during the night of April 12 a church bell never rang.

It was important to have a means to communicate to the public and a newspaper was the best way to do that so Andrew Johnson brought S.C. Mercer, a Union loyalist, from Louisville to edit a newspaper, The Daily Union; the first issue was on April 13. Two days after The Daily Union published its initial issue, Johnson had E.E. Jones, editor of the Banner, and James T. Bell, former editor of the Nashville Gazette, arrested and charged with treason, which caused the Banner to cease publication. This left Edward without a job and under suspicion from Union forces.

CHAPTER 25

On April 19 the Nashville Theatre opened; it was the old Adelphi Theatre and I invited Mrs. Monahan and Rachel to attend the opening night performance. I knew the owners, Mr. Duffield and Mr. Sands, and obtained tickets prior to the box office opening.

Mrs. Monahan declined—I thought she might, since she did not enjoy our last visit to the theatre—so Rachel and I, along with my sons Edward and Matthew, enjoyed the performance of the actors, although the company was smaller than previous companies. The War had an effect on the Nashville Theatre; no Northern stars—and the "stars" were all in the North—would come into this War zone. The large number of soldiers in Nashville made it easy to fill the theatre with a paying crowd, but those soldiers, many of whom were just farm boys with no experience watching plays, were rowdy and disruptive. Many of the foot soldiers—and not a few of the officers—tended to be drunk when they arrived, yelled at the actors on stage and started fights with others attending the play but Nashvillians were starved for entertainment and something to get our minds off the terrible War and occupation so the theatre was always full.

Rachel was clearly disgusted with the Union army's presence and bombarded me with questions about the officers and Governor Johnson, who stayed at the St. Cloud Hotel.

At the end of the evening, Edward and Matthew left us and as Rachel and I walked she was forceful in her desire to help the

Confederacy. She told me she knew other young ladies who wanted to help and they would try to gain information to communicate to the Southern army.

"And how do you propose to do that?" I asked. She answered with a sly smile as she hooked her arm in mine. I cautioned, "You've got to get a pass from the military to leave town and they're very strict with every man in town, demanding he sign a Loyalty Oath and explain where he's going and why."

"A woman has ways and abilities that a man does not have," she replied as she smiled at me. "But I'll need your help. Would you let me know about the conversations you hear in the St. Cloud while you are dining or with Union officers?"

I told her I would and she and Mrs. Monahan should also move into the St. Cloud. "We've talked about that," she said. "It doesn't seem safe with so many Union ruffians on the streets to be in a home in town." I told her I would speak to the manager as soon as possible to see if that could be arranged.

The next day, Rachel and Mrs. Monahan moved into a room at the St. Cloud.

CHAPTER 26

A few days later Robert, Edward, Matthew and I dined at the St. Cloud and Robert told me he could no longer ignore the War; he intended to join the Rebel army. Union troops had come to his farm on several occasions and taken chickens, cattle and two mules. They had raided his home, taken meats that were curing and his stock of vegetables.

I asked about the agreement he had with John Overton to own the farm but Robert said "I see no reason to continue farming. Those Feds are going to steal everything I grow. I've lost just about everything already—there's not much left."

Robert told me he had decided to join Colonel John Hunt Morgan's cavalry. I knew of Colonel Morgan, but had never met the man. Robert told me that Morgan had lived in Kentucky but when his state did not join the Confederacy he left and was sworn into the Confederate army as a Captain. At Shiloh he was promoted to Colonel and learned a valuable lesson: a small, light, mobile force was more effective than a large force fighting big battles. Morgan intended to recruit such a force and had met Robert. Morgan was serving under Generals Wheeler and Braxton but was going to strike out on his own.

Edward, Matthew and I sat in silence for a few moments before I asked, "When will you be joining Colonel Morgan?"

"Day after tomorrow," he said. "I have a horse and a rifle and Colonel Morgan said I'll need a pistol. I intend to buy one tomorrow."

"We'll be operating in Middle Tennessee," said Robert, "but it will be hard to send you letters or let you know my whereabouts because we'll be on the move." I said I understood and asked only that he send a letter when he could to let me know he was well. He said he would either send a letter or get a message to me through a network of Rebel loyalists. There were, according to Robert, an underground network of "friends" who helped the Confederate army and he had met several of them.

The conversation was light after Robert told me this and Edward and Matthew remained quiet for the rest of the meal. As we parted I shook his hand, wished him the best and gave him some money. He and Edward walked away together while Matthew headed in a different direction. I went back to my room at the St. Cloud and prayed he would be safe.

CHAPTER 27

Rachel informed me that young ladies she was acquainted with made it a point to be impertinent to Union soldiers. Many of those young ladies carried pistols and insulted Union officers to their faces. Rachel told me of several instances when young ladies turned their backs on a Union officer when the officer tried to converse. A few of the young ladies spit on Union soldiers and more than one young lady, in the company of Union officers, stated "Your absence, sirs, will be much better company to me than your presence."

Mr. Carter owned the St. Cloud and his daughter, Laura, who like Rachel was 20 years old, stood on the hotel's porch and spit on some Union solders. For this, she was sent to Governor Johnson's office in the Capitol. This was an awkward situation, since Governor Johnson was a guest at the hotel, but he just told her to "behave herself." When the defiant Miss Carter replied she would dance on his grave, Governor Johnson laughed and told her she would plant flowers instead. Governor Johnson told the Union soldiers who brought her to his office "you mustn't mind these little Rebels" and ordered them to let her go.

Rachel relayed this story to me and was giddy with excitement. "See," she said. "A young woman can get away with much more than a man can."

"Yes," I replied, "but honey attracts more bees." Rachel looked at me pensively and then replied, "Yes, I believe you're right," and seemed to withdraw into herself, silent for a long period, which was unlike her. Finally, she smiled and said "honey can trap bees when they land in it."

The next day Edward came to my room and informed me that he had purchased a horse from the Belle Meade Plantation and joined Colonel Forrest's cavalry. I shook his hand and congratulated him but in my heart I felt a tinge of regret, concerned about his fate. I wished him well. When I informed Rachel about Edward her eyes glowed and she swelled with pride. She and Edward were close to the same age and I wondered again about the future of those two, who seemed to enjoy each other's company.

CHAPTER 28

The influx of Union soldiers led to a demand for restaurants and saloons, which were soon established, as well as sutler stores which sold provisions and supplies to soldiers. Shopkeepers and peddlers from the north moved into Nashville and set up retail establishments but farmers in the area were reluctant to plant crops because armies often marched over their fields. Both armies were merciless to farmers in the countryside; they tore down rail fences and used them for firewood, seized beef, chickens and other farm animals, and destroyed crops as they foraged for food for themselves and their animals. If there was a vacant building in Nashville, the Union army seized it.

The Union army controlled most of Middle Tennessee south of Nashville, extending into Huntsville and Florence, Alabama. After the Battle of Shiloh, the Federals were strong west of Nashville because of cavalry raids but from Lebanon, about 30 miles east of Nashville on eastward, the Confederates had control of the countryside.

The Belle Meade Plantation, home of William G. Harding, was guarded by four Union soldiers. Rachel told me that even though Harding was the bane of Unionists—he was a die-hard Southerner—the plantation was protected by Union soldiers. However, according to Rachel, the soldiers took mules, poultry, sweet potatoes, deer and buffalo from the farm. Those Union soldiers also took liberties with the slave women.

Rachel managed to keep in touch with a wide variety of people and gathered news from all of them. I often wondered how she could find out so much, although she was quite sociable and loved to talk. Sometimes she traveled with a group of ladies to a Southern army camp where they passed along messages and information about the Union army in Nashville. Mrs. Monahan was always concerned about Rachel's travels but the young lady was determined to help the Rebel army.

By June, 1862, there were virtually no wooden fences left in or around Nashville; soldiers had used them for firewood. There were no horses—soldiers confiscated them—nor was there hay or corn to feed animals; farmers had no food for themselves. Most of the best buildings in Nashville had been taken over by the Federals and used as military hospitals or storehouses and the streets were filthy. The damage was not done by military battles but by the presence of Union soldiers who occupied the city. Middle Tennessee became the strategic center for the Union army's campaign in the western theatre of the Civil War; it also became the breadbasket of the Union army.

CHAPTER 29

I first met Andrew Johnson when he was in the House of Representatives and knew him during the 1840s. I came to know him better when he was Governor of Tennessee from 1853 to 1857. I dined with Governor Johnson several times at the St. Cloud and found him to be a good conversationalist but a rather rigid thinker. He lacked the skills of tact and diplomacy and while some may have seen greatness in him, I must confess that I did not. He was a "small" man when challenged, never able to rise above perceived slights to grasp a bigger picture.

There is no doubt he was in a very difficult position as Military Governor of Tennessee. His views on the Union—and against the secessionists—were diametrically opposed to most of those living in Nashville. Johnson's firm belief was that the Rebels were wrong and the Union should remain preserved as one, which was also the view of the government in Washington. There was a War being fought over the two conflicting ideas of a solid Union verses the right to secede and Johnson was caught in the middle.

Johnson reacted with stern measures to assure loyalty to the Union. I'm sure if he had been too lenient towards Southern sympathizers in Nashville, the city would have been in chaos and ungovernable. Still, he could have been a bit more lenient than he was. His insistence on the Loyalty Oath—and punishment of those who did not take it—seemed unnecessary and at odds with a way to win the hearts and minds of citizens.

There are men who do not possess the attributes or qualities of greatness but who yearn to be considered great and I felt that Governor Johnson was one of those. There are men who want respect and feel they gain it from an administrative position they hold rather than deeds they do or qualities they possess. There are administrative positions held by men that demand respect—and Military Governor of Tennessee was certainly one of those—but Johnson himself did not earn the respect of the people of Nashville. A man must possess more than an administrative appointment to gain enduring admiration and respect.

There were about 10,000 Federal troops in Nashville by late spring, 1862 and every day groups of them went into the countryside around Nashville and took horses, cows, pigs, chickens, corn and whatever else they wanted from farmers who could do nothing but watch helplessly. Citizens inside the city felt the effects of an occupying army as well; you had to get permission to travel, conduct business or even send letters. The Feds wanted to hurt the Rebels any way they could.

The citizens of Nashville hated Federal troops in their city, but the troops also resented being in a Southern city and in their bitterness the soldiers blamed Southerners for the War. This led Federal troops to justify their destruction of anything belonging to those who sympathized with the South. It was a difficult pill to swallow as some of the wives and daughters of wealthy men who had either joined the Confederate army or openly supported the Confederate cause were forced to a level of poverty they were unaccustomed to and had to search and beg for food and housing. Many of those women had been in the social elite of Nashville;

now they found themselves no better than a poor farmer's wife and daughter.

There were Rebel guerrillas outside Nashville which were a constant source of trouble for the Feds. I heard stories about Colonel Morgan's raiders who constantly attacked Federal soldiers and disrupted activities. The action of guerrillas led to a constant stream of rumors the Rebel army was prepared to strike Nashville, re-capture the city and get rid of the Federal troops. Those rumors circulated constantly and gave an abiding hope that hardships inflicted on Nashville citizens by the Union army would one day soon be over.

The city and countryside were full of local Southern loyalists—"secesh" they were called—and Governor Johnson felt threatened by them. There were soldiers on horses riding up and down the streets of Nashville day and night, stopping and searching citizens and making arrests so Johnson could feel safe.

I knew Robert was with Morgan's raiders and heard news about him occasionally from Rachel, who had an effective grapevine that kept her informed about the Rebel army. Rachel had visited Robert when she traveled outside the city with a group of young ladies to Colonel Morgan's camp, but did not tell me any particulars and it was agreed that I would not ask; still, it was good to know he was alive and well. Rachel always spoke well of Robert and was proud that he served the Southern cause.

CHAPTER 30

In May former Governor Neill S. Brown was arrested for treason but took the Oath of Allegiance a few days later and was paroled. That same day, the Grand Jury indicted eight citizens for conspiracy; among the eight were James Childress, brother of Mrs. James K. Polk and David McGavock, who was arrested for concealing Confederate arms on his farm. Several bankers were arrested, including Daniel Carter, whose son was in the Confederate army. About a month later Carter was paroled and signed the Loyalty Oath.

John M. Lea, brother-in-law to John Overton, petitioned the Governor for Overton to return to his plantation in Nashville, saying he would use his influence to halt resistance to Federal authority. The sticking point was that Overton refused to take the Oath, although he pledged to live as if he was bound by it. Governor Johnson denied the plea but said he would grant permission for Overton to return "upon the strictist terms." Nobody quite knew what that meant but everyone suspected that Overton would have been a marked man if he had returned. Overton apparently thought so too because he declined and remained in the deep South.

Governor Johnson continued to believe there was a strong undercurrent of Union support in Nashville and that he could tap into this undercurrent and create a groundswell of support for the Federal government. This was the reason he allowed the election for Judge of the Circuit Court in late May. The problem was that Johnson deluded himself into believing in this underlying Union sentiment in the midst of the Confederacy where most citizens supported the Southern cause so he was shocked when the secessionist candidate won. This angered Johnson to the point that he declared he would never allow a secessionist to hold any public office so the victor was never sworn in.

Johnson believed that when bankers, insurance men, ministers, doctors and other civic leaders signed the Loyalty Oath, they would lead the way for every citizen to sign the Oath so he counted it as a triumph when Daniel Carter signed. Johnson was rather heavy-handed in getting citizens to sign the Oath. He controlled the Common Council, which passed an ordinance mandating all businessmen must pay a privilege tax in order to operate their business. The catch was that a receipt for the paid tax would not be issued until the businessman took the Loyalty Oath. There was also an ordinance passed against "seditious talk," which was defined as "any comment that might discourage support for the Union." It didn't take much for any group of words to be labeled "seditious talk" by Union enforcers.

I signed the Loyalty Oath to protect my sons but I did not tell Rachel.

CHAPTER 31

West Tennessee was heavily secessionist but in early June Fort Pillow fell, which opened the Mississippi for Federal gunboats to capture Memphis. In the Nashville area, Colonel Morgan continued to wreak havoc and kept Union soldiers nervous; Morgan and his cavalry appeared without warning, shot Federal pickets, took prisoners and then disappeared. Those raids instilled optimism in Nashville that Rebels would re-take the city, which tended to create an atmosphere where Union soldiers took revenge on the civilian population.

In an effort to recruit Nashvillians for the Union Army, Governor Johnson offered $100 and 160 acres of land—but there were few takers. This was a setback for Johnson, who again underestimated the loyalty Nashvillians had for the Confederacy. He also over-estimated the number of Unionists in Nashville; he thought they would be a source of strength for him.

Johnson was upset that three prominent Nashvillians he had arrested and sent to Fort Mackinac in Michigan had been treated well when they stopped in Detroit for several days. The trio, which included William Harding, dined at one of Detroit's finest hotels, walked the streets and visited places of amusement as they rode around Detroit in a carriage. Johnson intended the imprisonment of those three to be a deterrent for others with secessionist sympathies but this treatment seemed to make a mockery of his rule.

CHAPTER 32

True love blooms in the strangest places; in June a local girl, Laura Carlin married a Union army officer. The wedding was considered scandalous in Nashville; it was outrageous for a Nashville girl to marry a member of the enemy! Rachel did not hold back her venom when she gave me this news.

Churches and pastors had a mixed fate. The pastor of First Baptist Church informed Johnson he could not take the Oath and was arrested and sent to prison. The First Baptist Church on Summer Street, the Second Baptist Church on Cherry Street and the Spring Street Baptist Church closed early in 1862 and those buildings were claimed by the Union army, which used them as hospitals but Christ Church Episcopal held services throughout the War without interference.

Citizens wanted schools re-opened but school buildings were used as military hospitals so churches offered classes. On July the Fourth a 34 gun salute at the Capitol and ringing church bells greeted citizens. There was a military parade through downtown, speeches and ice cream, cake and apples, but few houses flew the Union flag and few citizens took part in the parade. A large number of Negroes did follow the parade and remained at the Capitol during the speech but most Rebel households ignored the event.

The constant hope of Nashvillians, and fear of Unionists, was that Nashville would be attacked by Confederate forces and in July the Rebs were hopeful and Feds were nervous because of news that Colonel Forrest's cavalry had left Chattanooga for Middle Tennessee. General John C. Breckenridge's infantry was also reportedly headed in the general direction of Nashville and Federal soldiers set about building fortifications to defend the city against attack and set out pickets and road patrols around the city. Union reinforcements were sent to the city and Governor Johnson pleaded for citizen volunteers to defend the city—about 200 answered his call—and vowed he would rather burn the city to the ground than surrender it to Confederate forces.

The city was noisy as fortifications were erected and cannons were placed so they could be turned on the city if it was overrun. While Nashvillians waited for Confederate forces to attack, reports came that Colonel Morgan's guerilla cavalry was wreaking havoc in Kentucky. Colonel Forrest captured Murfreesboro, about 30 miles south of Nashville, and more Federal reinforcements arrived. The roads leading into Nashville were barricaded by wagons fastened together with chains in anticipation of an attack by Forrest.

On July 21 and 22 Colonel Forrest led his cavalry on raids close to the city that destroyed railroad bridges and captured Union soldiers as prisoners. Forrest made it to the Hermitage, former home of Andrew Jackson, as Union soldiers slept with their arms and citizens anticipated a full-fledged battle for Nashville to erupt at any moment. That did not happen; instead, Forrest withdrew to Chattanooga as Federal reinforcements continued to arrive.

Rachel told me she had seen Edward when she and some other ladies visited Forrest's troops with letters and supplies and he had given her a letter. She handed me the sealed envelope and I opened it. The letter was short and read "Dear Father, I am unable to reveal much but want you to know that I am safe and am involved in a great and noble cause. I hope to see you soon but do not know when that will be. I must keep plans and where I am secret but please know that wherever I am and whatever I do I think often of you. Your loving son, Edward."

That letter did not say much and yet it spoke volumes to me. I put the letter in my inside coat pocket and read it numerous times in my room. You cannot imagine the joy a father feels when a son he has not seen for a period of time sends a letter. It is the most wonderful, heartfelt feeling a father can have.

Meanwhile, in Kentucky Colonel Morgan stopped trains and sent them back to Nashville. Travel restrictions for Nashville citizens were tightened; in order to enter or leave the city, a pass was required and only those who had taken the Loyalty Oath were issued passes. Union soldiers were required to wear their uniforms and have a pass if they were in the city. The threat of Forrest led Union occupiers to build stockades at every bridge.

Governor Johnson continued to live at the St. Cloud Hotel and ate in the hotel's public dining room, where I often saw him. He did not live in palatial splender; his bed filled half of his narrow bedroom.

CHAPTER 33

The Nashville Theatre closed for a week in July, then reopened; Mr. Duffield was the sole owner when it opened and his biggest problem was selecting plays that entertained the common soldier while, at the same time, did not offend the cultured citizens of Nashville who were regular theatre-goers.

Many of the Union officers appreciated more sophisticated fare, but the average foot soldier wanted rowdy entertainment with lots of pretty girls, especially if those girls were not adverse to showing a good amount of their bare legs to the crowd.

I took Rachel one evening and it was rather embarrassing; the decorum of the theatre was missing and I had to question the morals of most of the crowd. Still, Nashvillians needed—even demanded—entertainment to relieve the daily burden of being occupied.

One thing I noticed about those evenings with Rachel was that it fired her emotions to do even more against the Union army when she saw the behavior of Union troops, and yet she could be quite charming around young Union officers. There had been other young ladies who fell in love and married a young Union officer—the heart trumps the mind every day—and it would not have been a complete surprise if Rachel found a young Union officer who caused her to forget the color of his uniform. It had happened to a few other young ladies in Nashville, so it was not out of the question.

On July 31, Brigadier General Forrest celebrated his forty-first birthday by attacking Murfreesboro. He captured over a thousand Federal soldiers and destroyed the depot containing supplies and destroyed the railroad bridges of the Nashville and Chattanooga railroad. This "Battle of Murfreesboro," which began at dawn, ended in late afternoon.

Governor Johnson continued to worry about an attack on Nashville so more defense works were built around Nashville by slaves and contraband slaves who fled their owners. Forts were commissioned and Federal officers required slave owners to supply slaves for this work. However, slave owners had contracts to provide food for men and animals and needed their slaves to fulfill those contracts, which caused a conflict.

In August, Colonel Morgan's cavalry struck Gallatin, about 30 miles north of Nashville, and captured Federal troops without firing a shot. Morgan's soldiers captured a locomotive and drove it into a pile of crossties in a tunnel; the resulting fire and debris blocked the tunnel. Morgan's troops set fire to a train with 40 railroad cars and destroyed Union supplies, then burned a bridge about six miles south of Gallatin and captured the bridge guards. Those actions cut off Union supplies and troops coming into Nashville from Louisville as news spread that Colonel Morgan planned to attack Nashville and Governor Johnson would be sent to Alabama when Nashville was captured. News of Morgan's escapades caused Union forces to go to Gallatin to capture Morgan and his raiders but the Feds were defeated and their officer was captured by the elusive Morgan.

Another contingent of Union troops then went to Gallatin in pursuit of Morgan but the Rebel leader wasn't there; the Feds arrested over a hundred citizens and charged them with aiding and abetting Morgan. When news of those arrests reached Morgan, he led his cavalry to Gallatin and overtook the Feds, freed the captured prisoners, and attacked Federal forces in Edgefield. The skirmish lasted for about three hours, then Morgan retreated into the countryside. The raiders were gone but the threat remained as Union soldiers continually feared Morgan.

Morgan and his raiders continued to be a menace to Union forces in Nashville and inspired hope amongst Rebel sympathizers. Morgan's exploits created a major problem for the Federal army: How to protect the L&N railroad that transported troops and supplies between Louisville and Nashville.

CHAPTER 34

It was almost midnight when I was awakened by a knock on the door. I sat up in bed and noticed a paper had been slid under my door. I got out of bed and picked it up; it said "Breakfast 7 a.m. at City Hotel." I wondered about the note but knew I'd be there.

When I walked into the lobby of the City Hotel I was met by a young lady I did not know who greeted me with a smile and said, "I've got a seat for you." She led me into the eating area and seated me with a group of soldiers dressed in Union uniforms and bid me sit down. I resolved to act as natural as I could and took my seat.

"Good morning," said one of the soldiers, then another said, "it's good to see you" and I recognized Robert's voice. I was taken aback, unsure at first if this could be true, but I looked into Robert's face and could not help but smile. "We're only in town for a short while," he said. "We had to make a delivery."

"I see," I said. "And I hope the goods were delivered safely." "Yes," he said, "quite safe."

Amidst a general discussion Robert told me he had gone with Morgan into Kentucky where they captured Union cavalry, a supply depot and Colonel Morgan had issued a proclamation inviting Kentuckians to join the Confederates. He said they posted proclamations in a number of towns—Morgan had quite a few printed-and Morgan led them into Frankfort, the capital of Kentucky. Robert said the raiders had been supplied with guns, ammunition and horses in Kentucky.

Morgan was alerted that a Union force planned to capture him so he sent telegrams to several towns that he planned to visit. That misled Union forces—the telegrams were fake—and allowed his troops to spend time in Georgetown, resting. They needed the rest; riding with Morgan meant long days in the saddle and constant movement.

On their way back to Tennessee, Morgan's group captured several hundred more prisoners—their total in the Kentucky venture was over 1,200 prisoners—but Morgan had them paroled because he could not be mobile with all of those prisoners.

I asked about casualties and Robert answered "about a hundred," which caused me grave concern. "At least you are safe," I said, and Robert looked out the window, but he did not answer.

We only spent about 20 minutes at breakfast when one of the other soldiers said "we have to go." The others quickly got up, Robert nodded at me, smiled, and they walked out the door.

CHAPTER 35

On the evening of August 23 Rachel and I went to the Nashville Theatre and heard a wonderful musical performance by the band of the Ninth Indiana Regiment. They played a marvelous selection of tunes, from lively to slower numbers. Rachel and I did not talk while the music played; she had a dreamy look in her eyes as she put her head back and was swept away by the music, even though it was played by Union soldiers.

Rachel told me she heard that General Bragg's forces might be headed towards Nashville to attack the city; the buzz had come from several of her young lady friends who visited soldiers in that army, which was in Chattanooga. She knew General Buell's army was in Huntsville and he planned to move his troops from Northern Alabama towards Nashville if an attack was imminent. She also heard that Buell's soldiers were hungry, a result of successful Rebel attacks on trains carrying supplies to the army.

Rachel and I conducted these conversations in whispers, lest anyone overhear us. We walked with her left arm in the crook of my right arm and she told me she had something for me and with that put her right hand on my right bicep. I put my hand over her's as she slowly slid her hand out and then put it on mine. She kept it that way until we were in front of the St. Cloud Hotel, then moved it away. I took the paper that was in my left hand and, appearing to adjust my cuff, slipped the paper up my right shirt sleeve. "Give this to a boy," she said, "and don't look at it."

I went to my room and waited for a knock, which came about ten minutes later. A young boy—he could not have been more than eight—stood at the door with a small, tin box. "I'm delivering your tea," he said and I took the box and put the paper inside, burying it underneath the loose tea leaves.

"Thank you, sir," he said, and left quickly. Chapter 36

Living in Nashville became quite uncomfortable—and even dangerous—for native citizens. There were soldiers and Northern spies everywhere and everyone was required to take the Loyalty Oath. The Oath was odious; it stated:

I solemnly swear, that I will henceforth support the Constitution of the United States and defend it against the assaults of all its enemies; that I will hereafter be, and conduct myself as a true and faithful citizen of the United States, freely and voluntarily claiming to be subject to all the duties, and obligations, and entitled to all the rights and privileges of such citizenship; that I ardently desire the suppression of the present insurrection and rebellion against the Government of the United States, the success of its armies and the defeat of all those who oppose them, and that the Constitution of the United States, and all laws and proclamations, made in pursuance thereof, may be speedily and permanantly established and enforced over all the people, States and Territories thereof; and further, that I will hereafter heartily aid and assist all loyal people in the accomplishment of these results. So help me God.

Rachel and I had discussed the Loyalty Oath and she was adamantly against it when we first discussed it. A few nights later, I saw her in front of the St. Cloud with her mother and she greeted me, "Mr. Duncan, would you like to take a walk with me? My mother is tired." I agreed and we walked, arm in arm, for several blocks.

"I believe you should take the Loyalty Oath," she said coyly. "But I thought you were against it," I replied. "I am," she said, "but there's a value in taking the Oath—there's no danger of being arrested."

"How can you be arrested if you're doing nothing wrong?" I asked, smiling. She smiled back at me, "These Northern soldiers and the Governor don't care if you're doing anything wrong or not—or whether you're a good citizen or not," she said. "All that matters is the Loyalty Oath."

"I see," I said. "But I don't want to live a lie; I'm not a hypocrite," I said.

"Have you seen what the Loyalty Oath says," she asked.

Indeed I had; in fact, I had a copy of it with me so we went over it line by line.

"'I solemnly swear, that I will henceforth support the Constitution of the United States and defend it against the assaults of all its enemies,'" said Rachel, "and that means that you believe in the Constitution, which states that each State is a voluntary member of the Union. There's no problem with that is there?"

"No," I said. "I don't see that there is."

She continued, "'that I will hereafter be, and conduct myself as a true and faithful citizen of the United States, freely and voluntarily claiming to be subject to all the duties, and obligations, and entitled to all the rights and privileges of such citizenship.' Since Tennessee has joined the Confederacy, that means that we have dual citizenship. We don't have to give up our citizenship of the United States in order to be citizens of the Confederacy. You can be a citizen of England and the United States," she said.

Well, I thought that was stretching it quite a bit—but I allowed the possibility of being a citizen of two different countries.

"'That I ardently desire the suppression of the present insurrection and rebellion against the Government of the United States' means that we want this War to be over with. And we do, don't we?" I nodded.

"The success of its armies and the defeat of all those who oppose them, and that the Constitution of the United States, and all laws and proclamations, made in pursuance thereof, may be speedily and permanently established and enforced over all the people, States and Territories thereof." She finished that sentence and looked at me. "How are you going to interpret that?" I asked.

"I think that means that if the army, or rather an army...well," she said after a pause. "I believe that you can say you agree with most of it and majority rules. So that last line, 'and further, that I will hereafter heartily aid and assist all loyal people in the accomplishment of these results. So help me God' is a nice ending because we are all loyal people."

Sweet Rachel; she wanted those words to twist and turn in her favor and she did her best to make them do so. As for me, I had signed the Oath soon after it was issued to protect my sons, two of whom were serving in the Rebel army. I faced a wicked choice and resolved to compromise, although there was a slight bitter taste in my mouth when I signed the document. I did not want to leave Nashville because I wanted to remain in Nashville and see my sons and I thought that might be the best way to do so.

CHAPTER 37

In Nashville, Governor Johnson continued to crack down on citizens, allowing no one to leave the city without taking the Loyalty Oath. There were a number of arrests of citizens in July and August and a shipment of shoes and clothing gathered for the Confederate army was captured. Rachel was upset when she found out about this; she knew a group of ladies were secretly gathering supplies for Confederate soldiers and wondered how they would get them out of the city.

Most of the citizens of Nashville lived in poverty; the families of Union volunteers received cash stipends but the rest of the population was out of work, money, food and fuel. Fortunately, the St. Cloud Hotel always had food and fuel because a number of Union officers stayed and ate there.

By September, the cost of everything was inflated. Those who had wealth kept it in currency, securities, gold, jewelry or other valuables that could be safe. The Union soldiers took food and wood but left valuables alone. Throughout the city, citizens roamed around during the day or lived in run-down buildings. The plantation owners who remained continued to live in their mansions but were constantly threatened by vigilantes and guerrillas. Inside the city, citizens feared arrest and abuse from Federal forces.

Governor Johnson continued to believe that white citizens in Middle Tennessee were Unionists at heart but had been tricked into endorsing secession by the aristocratic elite. Johnson wanted to reestablish civil government but first needed to purge the disloyal elements of the population. His major weapon was the Loyalty Oath, which was odious to those who felt themselves to be law-abiding citizens whose only sin was sympathy for the South.

The Governor did not understand the deep attachment a person has for their homeland.

CHAPTER 38

During our stroll one Sunday afternoon in September, Rachel told me that Mrs. Elizabeth Harding sent two letters to Governor Johnson. In the first letter, she offered a bond of any amount he chose to allow her husband to come back to Belle Meade in order to make a decision about whether or not to stay. She felt that taking the Oath for the parole would be taking the Oath of Allegiance. She and General Harding had known Governor Johnson for a long time, since before he was Governor of Tennessee.

In the second letter, Rachel said, Mrs. Harding was mad and poured out her invective on Governor Johnson. Rachel said she and some of her friends had visited Belle Meade and Mrs. Harding was incensed that Union troops had taken hundreds of wagon loads of hay, corn, oats, wheat and other things and never given her a receipt. She had cooperated with the Union army, given them sixty tons of hay, but soldiers still took her horses, killed her poultry as well as her slave's chickens, and took the vegetables she had stored for the winter. They also took 22 of her male Negro slaves and nine mules.

Mrs. Harding said her female slaves were not safe and that Federal soldiers had taken liberties and threatened them and those Negro women ran to Mrs. Harding for protection. Soldiers took money from the Negroes and threatened to kill them. Those soldiers demanded her slaves give them all the milk and butter and a soldier shot Bob, her favorite male slave. Mrs. Harding said that Union soldiers had taken all her corn and oats and shot two Cashmere goats that General Harding paid $1,000 each for and just left them dead on the ground. The Hardings lost most of their deer and buffalo to those soldiers as well as all their sweet potatoes. They'd even robbed the slaves' cabins but Mrs. Harding stopped them from taking a stallion belonging to General Harding—worth about $1,500. She told them the horse was too good for use as a cavalry horse when they told her they were taking it to give as a gift to one of their officers.

General Thomas had written a note saying her place was protected but it meant nothing to those soldiers, who were brutes and animals. Finally, General Thomas sent some other soldiers to protect her and that stopped the foraging.

CHAPTER 39

Rachel and I were at the Nashville Theatre on an evening in September when a group of Union soldiers from Ohio, unable to find seats in the crowded theatre, stormed upstairs to the Negro gallery and began beating the Negroes. It was a terrible uproar, rather brutal and bloody and within ten minutes every single Negro in the theatre had been beaten by the soldiers and thrown out of the theatre. The Union soldiers were like animals; they threw Negroes down the stairs and bloodied them.

After the play, the soldiers went into the streets and grabbed every Negro and beat them unmercifully. It was a sickening display of brutality and caused the Provost to forbid foot soldiers from coming into the city unless they were on duty. The theatres were shut down and remained closed until November and all citizens had a 9 p.m. curfew.

CHAPTER 40

As Mrs. Monahan, Rachel and I dined one night the conversation turned to divided families in Nashville. Those families went through terrible ordeals as a husband might be a Unionist while his wife was loyal to the Confederacy; that was the case with Joshua Pearl, a Unionist who was Chairman of the Board of Education who fled North during the War while his son served as a soldier in the Confederacy and his wife was a Southern sympathizer.

Andrew Jackson, Jr. was a Unionist but his wife, sons and nephews remained loyal to the South and Daniel Smith Donelson, a member of one of Nashville's oldest families, served as a General in the Confederate army while Andrew Jackson Donelson was a Unionist. Francis Fogg, a leader in the local movement for public education and a lay official in Christ Church Episcopal, was a Unionist but his wife and son were Southern sympathizers; his son, Henry died as a Confederate soldier. Attorney Balie Peyton, Jr.'s father was a Unionist but Balie served as an officer in the Confederate army.

It is difficult to love someone when their views on an important subject or issue are opposite yours. For husbands and wives, this sometimes meant an icy resolve where subjects were not brought up or discussed. In some cases, there was no communication; the two lived under the same roof, but where they once shared a a deep love for each other, now they only shared an obligation to remain married, a commitment to be accepted as a married couple yet aligned with differing factions within the community.

A wealthy married couple sometimes chose separate residences, separated by miles. The couple was still married but did not have to face each other every night and day. Others had separate bedrooms or even separate areas of the house where they resided.

How can you truly love someone when you hold a deep contempt for their views? The best that can be hoped for is a toleration of the other as a human being with the same courtesies extended that would be given to any other human being. It is especially difficult with children you have brought into the world. You wonder how they can see things so differently from you when they were raised under your roof.

For those in divided families, a coldness tended to dominate the relations between family members. A love was buried deeply in one towards the other but there could never be the full joy that comes when hearts, souls and minds are united. Each day, the love within a divided family is tested and becomes weaker with each passing event that cheers one member and frustrates or disappoints another.

A sense of disbelief pervades the internal dynamics of a divided family, the sense of "how can they believe what they believe?" or even "how dare they think that way?" There is a never ending heartache within divided families, a struggle to be compassionate and caring when each family member wants to see the dissenting member brought to their knees and to their senses, to have it proven to them, once and for all, that they are wrong.

People don't admit they are wrong, although they allow events that conform to their views to prove them right. Instead, they reinterpret the facts, find a new way to look at an outcome that alters their views and allows them to feel comfortable their beliefs remain true, although perhaps misunderstood. Few say or believe "I was wrong" but many allow they have been misled or wandered into a view that was deficient of a knowledge needed to form a better opinion at the time.

A husband and wife whose political views are polar opposite live in a world of unspoken thoughts, a life where some subjects are not even acknowledged, much less discussed. If they remain married and live in the same home, they live with a truce, an avoidance of expressing their true thoughts and feelings in front of the other with an acceptance their life together will never again capture the joy of their young love. They can only hope their marriage will bring a comfort in old age, a warmth of shared years that ends in having someone to share the fading light of life as their twilight drops into the darkness of death.

I knew that Matthew had sided with Unionists, although he never told me outright, but during our conversations I could discern his heart was with the Union. Rachel knew it and had whispered it to me. I was silent when she told me; I wanted to preserve my love for Matthew. A father loves his son no matter what the son does or believes, but it hurt me that Matthew and I did not see eye to eye; moreover, that our family was divided. When Rachel talked of Matthew she was careful not to disparage him, but she could not hide her feelings and avoided mentioning his name. Matthew kept his job at the telegraph office because he was loyal to the Union, and sometimes he dropped by my room and gave me news he heard about General Forrest.

Robert was another matter. It hurt to know that Morgan's raids caused so many to be hurt or killed. I agreed with Robert's sympathies but I did not want to contemplate the consequences of his actions.

CHAPTER 41

The dining room at the St. Cloud was nearly empty except for Mrs. Monahan, Rachel and me as we ate our dinner one evening. Rachel informed me that when General Buell led his troops through Nashville they were on their way to Kentucky. During four days in September Union soldiers marched through Nashville, followed by thousands of blacks who attached themselves to the army.

General George Thomas took command of Federal troops in and around Nashville in September and marched to Bowling Green in pursuit of General Bragg's army. Rachel said Governor Johnson was upset because so many Union soldiers had left Nashville.

At times the St. Cloud dining room was full and people had to wait in line to find a seat but on this particular evening the tables were nearly empty. It felt as if the Union army had abandoned Nashville and I began our conversation by asking if Rachel had heard any news about the Southern army taking advantage of this situation. Rachel said she had been in the dining room when General Thomas showed another officer paper—his orders—he kept in his pocket which stated, "If Bragg's army is defeated, Nashville is safe; if not, it is lost."

Rachel became acquainted with Governor Johnson and said she overheard him on several occasions complaining about Buell. It was clear that Johnson disliked General Buell and even expressed the belief he was a traitor to the Union cause. Rachel said she and two other young ladies were conversing with some young Federal lieutenants one evening when one revealed he heard General Buell say that, from a military point of view, holding Nashville was not of great importance and the city should have been abandoned or evacuated three months ago.

General Buell also said, after meeting with the Governor, that Nashville was occupied for political—not military—considerations. The officers told the young ladies that Governor Johnson "had his ears boxed" when Buell confronted him about what he heard of Johnson's accusations.

Rachel said that Confederate forces currently around Nashville were not large or particularly strong and they could make no headway when they attempted to attack outlying Federal troops around Nashville. She said Union officers vastly overestimated the number of troops with Colonel Morgan, before adding, "I'm sure Robert is safe."

Rachel revealed that her mother had made a pair of pants for me. I was surprised and demurred at first before Rachel placed her hand on my arm and said, "there's a secret pocket on the outside of each leg." I raised an eyebrow when I looked at her; she smiled and continued.

She told me the young boy who came to my room is known as "Billy" and he is an important part of her work for the Rebels. If I needed to meet someone, such as Billy, I should do so inside the Episcopal Church.

There were times when Rachel needed for me to have a letter; she passed these by holding the paper in her hand, putting her hand on my arm and then me putting my hand under her's to get the paper. When we parted, I needed to slip the paper into the pocket slit in the side of my trousers. If I needed to give a letter to her, we reversed this and I held the paper against my arm and she put her hand over mine. There were slit pockets in her dresses—she had several long, full dresses—and the paper would be slipped into a pocket.

We could do this because I had signed the Loyalty Oath, she said, but it was important that no Union soldier or spy see what we were doing; if we were caught, Rachel could be put into prison and I could be put in prison or shot—probably shot. And yet it seemed worth the risk.

After dinner we decided to practice our exchange using her handkerchief. It was a small white handkerchief and if anyone saw us making this exchange, there would be no harm—it was just a handkerchief. And so we strolled throughout the city streets that evening, conversing with one another in low tones and practicing our handoff. As for "Billy," Rachel told me that was the name she wanted him known by—it was obviously not his real name—and I would only see him in regards to messages to be carried. That was all I was to know. I was comfortable with that decision and amazed that Rachel, a beautiful young lady, could have such nerves of steel and a courage that belied a Southern Belle whose charms led young men to believe she was a helpless, giddy female.

Thus began my involvement in carrying messages. I never read any of them, only served as a go-between when needed.

CHAPTER 42

General Forrest was with his cavalry in Lavergne, about ten miles south of Nashville, and continued to challenge the Federal forces surrounding the city. Confederate Major Richard McCann led a cavalry unit located near Nolensville, just a few miles south of the city while another cavalry unit, commanded by Captain Frank McNairy was in the Franklin Road area, about ten miles south of the city.

I gave Rachel a letter for Edward; she said she would get it to him. I did not ask how she could do this but those young ladies always found a way to charm their way past young Union officers. A group of ladies often visited the Rebel army in the field when the underground network informed them where the soldiers were camped.

The citizens of Nashville were abuzz with rumors that Nashville was about to be captured by Southern forces and we would be freed. The truth was that Nashville was in a siege and not only could we not leave the city, we could not get reliable information about either Northern or Southern forces.

One evening as Rachel and I strolled along the streets of Nashville—it was necessary that we stroll often, even when we did not pass messages so we would not be suspicious when there were messages to pass—she told me that one of her young lady friends reported the Rebel army had sent troops to Tullahoma and Colonel Morgan's cavalry had moved towards Nashville to harass Union troops.

As she told me this, we saw Federal soldiers setting up barricades on the streets of Nashville and saw Union snipers standing on roofs of buildings. Rachel felt certain the Confederate army would enter Nashville and knew a number of women—including her mother—were hard at work preparing chicken breasts, cakes, custards and other goodies for the Rebel troops when they arrived.

We learned later that Confederate General Anderson presented a formal demand to General Negley to surrender the city and raise the white flag; General Negley refused to do so but the Rebels did not attack. There was still Rebel cavalry and guerillas outside Nashville—we heard reports of skirmishes quite often—but there was no Rebel invasion of Nashville and all the food lovingly prepared by those women would not go to any member of the Union army; however, Rachel and I enjoyed a picnic with some of the remaining food under a tree on a Sunday afternoon.

CHAPTER 43

Rachel was furious when she joined me for dinner one evening. She murmured "Who did it? Who turned them in?" before she revealed to me the story of two young men, John Kirkman and John P.W. Brown, who attempted to sneak out of town with forged permits and join the Rebel army. However, before they left a Union detective came to their home and arrested them. Somehow Union officials had learned of their plans.

The two young men were taken to the Provost Marshal, who put them in prison. Rachel let her anger simmer a bit longer before she brought some good news. There were 21 men, led by a Rebel spy—she did not name him—who crawled through muddy fields on a rainy night to join the Confederate army. The men were hidden at the home of Dr. John Rolfe Hudson, who helped the Southern government a great deal by hiding Rebels and providing information to Southern spies when he could.

There were several occasions when a Union officer, while dining at the St. Cloud, asked "How are your sons?" This always took me by surprise but I do not believe I ever revealed my surprise; I always answered something to the effect, "I hope they're doing well. I never see them and hope this War ends soon so families can get back together." I could not help but believe those officers knew more about my sons than I wanted them to know.

There were Union forces all around Nashville and it was difficult to leave the city without running into them. The only way to get through was a proper pass, although some occasionally snuck through Union lines. The popular style for young ladies was large, hoop skirts and a number of young ladies Rachel knew smuggled letters and medicines under their skirts to the Rebel army. Some of the women even managed to hide shoes, boots and supplies under their ample skirts. I knew that Rachel was one of those young ladies who occasionally visited the Rebel army with supplies, but I never asked specifics. However, she usually remained in Nashville and flirted with young Union lieutenants. Her friends decided that, since she did not have a young beau in the Confederate army, she would be more effective charming young Federals and getting information from them.

Rachel and her group of friends were not the only Rebel spies in Nashville; Mrs. Clara Judd was John Hunt Morgan's female spy while Dr. John Rolfe Hudson, whose home was near the penitentiary, spent much of his time aiding the Confederate army as a smuggler, spy and aide to escaped Confederate soldiers.

CHAPTER 44

By October, it was hard to find food in Nashville. The river was low, which kept boats from arriving, the railroad tunnel north of Gallatin was blocked by Confederate soldiers, and the army and citizens had to depend upon local farms for food. Mr. Carter always managed to find food for the St. Cloud Hotel—I know he acquired quite a bit from Henry Compton's farm, about four and a half miles south of the city—since Governor Johnson and Union officers stayed or ate at the St. Cloud.

Rachel often passed me "letters"—although they were usually folded pieces of paper—but I was never to look at the papers that Rachel passed to me or that I passed on to Billy. I knew Rachel often drew maps of Federal defenses in Nashville and I, too, sometimes sketched out lines of defense I observed. If I overheard some interesting information while dining, or even through casual conversations with Federal officers—I always made it a point to be friendly and inviting to everyone—I jotted it on a piece of paper and handed it to Rachel or arranged to meet Billy.

Rachel and I cultivated the habit of strolling together arm and arm almost every evening after dinner. I enjoy a good walk after dinner; it helps me digest my food and is a pleasant way to pass the time after dinner and table conversation. In that way, we remained consistent in our behavior so when there was information to pass along, we did not look suspicious.

One evening, during our stroll, I told Rachel I heard that Ogilvie Byron Young had a pair of boots made with hollow heals to carry papers and wondered if I should do the same. She was surprised by this news— she always knew more than I did about the comings and goings in Nashville—and said she thought it was a good idea and, further, wished she could have a pair of boots as well. That was very unladylike, but I said I would have some boots made for myself.

Two weeks later I received a pair of boots with hollow heels; I could slip the bottom off and hide papers in there. Sometimes Billy came to my room and collected my boots "to polish" and took them somewhere. When he returned they had been "polished."

Rachel and I were not the only ones in Nashville collecting information about the Union army and sending it to the Rebels. Mrs. Edwin D. Payne and her sister Mrs. Napoleon B. Hyde, Miss Robbie Woodruff, Ann Patterson and her cousin Kate Patterson, all gathered information. Rachel had a group of young lady friends—there were seven of them and they liked that number because it was "lucky"—who gathered information and smuggled it out of Nashville. Those ladies smuggled a lot out of Nashville, usually hiding mail and even supplies under their dresses. We were fortunate the style of the day was long, full hoop skirts because women could hide a lot under those dresses. Since there were only men in the Union army, they were limited in their search of women and, of course, women took advantage of that fact. Claiming their "honor" was at stake, women, for the most part, avoided intrusive searches.

Women were more likely to obtain passes to travel outside Nashville to visit a husband, fiance, cousin, brother, uncle, father or any other relative—real or imagined—who was in the Rebel army or lived in another Southern city. There were well organized groups of spies in most Southern cities and they found a way to keep the Southern army supplied with information about the Northern invaders.

Some Nashville merchants spied, although they had taken the special Oath of Loyalty. However, the Board of Trade determined which goods were essential and those merchants were eligible to receive trade permits and bring in goods from outside Nashville. This allowed them to travel outside the confines of Nashville as well as carry messages to those outside the city.

There was turmoil and violence in Nashville during the Fall of 1862. In September, George Sloan, who owned a carriage factory on Market Street, was ambushed as he drove from his farm in Ashland City; he died the next day. A Union sympathizer was killed by Confederate guerrillas and a doctor was killed by Union soldiers after he did not stop when they shouted at him as he left Belle Meade. In October Adelicia Acklen's brother was arrested and kept in prison until he took the Loyalty Oath. The next day William Harding, owner of the Belle Meade plantation, arrived in Nashville after posting bond of $10,000.

On October 13, the Governor's wife, Eliza Johnson, arrived in Nashville; she had traveled by rail from her East Tennessee home accompanied by their son, Charles, daughter Mary Johnson Stover and Stover's husband, Daniel and their three children. They arrived safely after going through Knoxville, Chattanooga and Murfreesboro—all cities controlled by the Confederate army. General Forrest assured their safety when he allowed the party to travel under a flag of truce. The family settled in at 58 Cedar Street in a home which was seized in May for their use.

Johnson would not allow an election to be held and in October appointed eight aldermen and 16 councilmen for the city. That month General Negley called on citizens to surrender their firearms; the citizens gave him old, rusted guns.

CHAPTER 45

On a Sunday in November there was a riot started by drunken soldiers who broke windows and pillaged stores. This led the Provost of the city to ban the sale of liquor. Nashville was a dangerous, violent town, especially on Smokey Row where the prostitutes conducted their business and soldiers often got into drunken fights and were killed. It was said that more soldiers died on Smokey Row than died on a battlefield during the Civil War.

As I took my walk one day, I was confronted by a Union soldier who, while not totally drunk, obviously had been drinking. He railed at me, without my provoking him in any way, shouting "I believe these secessionists deserve whatever they get. They oughta all be shot and killed or hung. I went into a woman's house and demanded dinner. Well, why shouldn't I? She was eating good and I was on half rations. She was known secessh—her own son was in the Confederate army and she was proud of it. These people are strange. About two thirds of 'em are secessionist. Above all the city is full of whores and free Negroes and that ain't no damn good for nobody." I acknowledged the man with a touch of the brim of my hat and walked on.

CHAPTER 46

Hope springs eternal and Rebel sympathizers continued to believe that a Confederate attack on Nashville was imminent. Those hopes were bolstered in November when General—it was now General—Morgan raided Edgefield while General Forrest and his troops were outside Nashville, threatening the Union army.

The citizens of Nashville heard the sound of Confederate guns. General Forrest's troops were firing to cover General Morgan and his troops who came into the city from Gallatin in the North in an attempt to destroy freight cars at the railroad station at Edgefield. Forrest's artillery opened fire that morning and the guns at Fort Negley answered back. Around ten that morning the artillery stopped as General Negley, waiting on Franklin Pike to ambush Forrest and his troops, found himself driven back into the city by Forrest, who used all of his artillery in the fight.

Forrest and his troops killed a number of Union soldiers and took prisoners while losing only a few. The Federals had better luck against Morgan, whose early morning surprise attack was thwarted by Federal troops, although Morgan's troops burned eight railroad cars before they retreated back to Gallatin.

I wondered if Robert and Edward had a chance to meet during those raids and that question was answered that evening when, during our walk, Rachel said, "Leave your door unlocked this evening. You may receive visitors."

I had fallen asleep—it was about two in the morning—when the door opened quietly and Robert and Edward walked in. I woke up as they came towards the bed and Edward whispered, "We wanted to surprise you."

"You certainly did," I whispered. We kept our voices low as Robert told me that Morgan's group had been in Lexington, Kentucky to help General Bragg's army, who planned to invade that state. Robert spent about a month in and around Lexington and then Morgan led raids to harass Union forces moving back into Tennessee. General Morgan captured Lexington and took several hundred prisoners, then moved on to Bardstown and Elizabethtown and destroyed railroad tracks.

Edward revealed that General Buell's army returned to Nashville with a new commander, General William Rosecrans. A number of those Union troops fought against Bragg's army and stopped Bragg's invasion of Kentucky. Both armies retreated to Tennessee because General Rosecrans thought there would be a battle in Nashville; however, Bragg went to Murfreesboro to re-group before he attacked Nashville.

We talked for about an hour, then Robert and Edward slept on the floor until daylight, when they left.

As I walked the streets of Nashville it was obvious the Union army expected General Bragg to attack Nashville because soldiers were building earthworks and entrenchments in a long semi-circle around the south of the city. Those earthworks were built mostly by Negroes, pressed into labor by the army. There were four forts stationed around the southern edge of the city: Fort Negley on St. Cloud Hill, Fort Andrew Johnson was the State Capitol with fortifications, Fort Confiscation was on Jones Hill and Fort Casino was on Terry Hill. The forts had heavy seige guns ready to fire on Confederate troops. With these defensive works, Nashville became one of the most fortified cities in the nation.

CHAPTER 47

General Rosecrans established his headquarters in Nashville in November and the former Army of the Ohio was re-named the Army of the Cumberland. Rachel heard whispers that Rosecrans wanted to engage Bragg's army, which he thought was in Murfreesboro and Tullahoma, but Federal scouts could find no Rebels south of the city. She told me that some of Forrest's cavalrymen just outside the city were captured and sent to a prison camp. Interestingly, one of the soldiers had a brother in the Union army. I was anxious to know if Edward had been captured; several days later she told me he had not.

Parson Brownlow preached a fiery sermon one Sunday at the McKendree Methodist Church in downtown Nashville, across the street from the St. Cloud Hotel. The crowd cheered him as he railed against the Rebels and Rebel sympathizers. Brownlow also attacked his fellow Methodist ministers, calling them "scoundrels." Parson Brownlow was a man on fire against the Confederacy.

I stood in front of the St. Cloud and listened to the cheers.

Billy brought me a copy of a Philadelphia newspaper dated November 15—it was only three days old when I received it—and the paper contained an interesting article where Governor Johnson stated, "I told the President that General Buell would never enter and redeem the Eastern portion of this state. I do not believe he ever intended to, despite his promises to the President and others that he would."

Governor Johnson claimed that Bragg's army was marching towards Nashville and Buell's army "could meet Bragg and whip him with the greatest ease" but he was compelled to reveal "with deep regret, what I know and believe General Buell's policy to be. Instead of meeting and whipping Bragg where he is, it is his intention to occupy a defensive position and is now, according to best evidence I can obtain, concentrating all his forces upon Nashville, giving up all the country which we have had possession of South and East of this place, leaving the Union sentiment and Union men, who took a stand for the Governor, to be crushed out and utterly ruined by the Rebels, who will all be in arms upon the retreat of our army." Johnson alleged that "General Buell fears his own personal safety, and has concluded to gather the whole army at this point as a kind of body guard to protect and defend him without reference to the Union men who have been induced to speak out, believing that the Government would defend them."

"General Buell is very popular with the Rebels," proclaimed Johnson, "and the impression is that he is more partial to them than to Union men and that he favors the establishment of the Southern Confederacy. I will not assume that General Buell desires the establishment of a Southern Confederacy and a surrender of Tennessee to the Rebels, but will give it as my opinion, that, if he had designed to do so, he could not have laid down or pursed a policy that would have been more successful in the accomplishment of both these objectives."

Governor Johnson concluded his speech with "May God save my country from some of the Generals that have been conducting the War."

Well, I thought, this must be old news since General Rosecrans is now in charge of the Union army and General Thomas is in Nashville. Governor Johnson burned with revenge against General Buell, who he felt was sympathetic to the Confederate cause.

CHAPTER 48

An odious man was inflicted upon the citizens of Nashville in December. "Colonel" Truesdail was a self-named Colonel, but insisted that citizens address him with that honor. He was a selfish, greedy, conniving man, drunk with power, a bully on the streets who had an insatiable appetite to punish the citizens of Nashville while he enriched himself.

Truesdail was brought to Nashville by General Rosecrans to be the civilian chief of police, giving him wide-ranging authority to do whatever it took to stop smuggling, limit the activities of Rebel spies, conduct intelligence gathering, supervise counter-intelligence operations and police the loyalty of the citizens and the behavior of the troops.

I learned that Truesdail was born in the state of New York where he first became a merchant and then a railroad contractor. Before the War he superintended the construction of a railroad across the Isthumus of Panama where most of the laborers sent from the United States were killed, but Truesdail survived. After he returned to the United States, Truesdail continued his railroad construction business and built railroads around St. Louis. He also supervised the construction of the railroad line connecting New Orleans to Houston.

By the time the War began Truesdail was a wealthy man; he moved to Missouri and began an informal affiliation with the Union army, serving as railroad superintendant, beef supply contractor, director of secret police, army police chief, intelligence gatherer, mail contractor and newspaper and magazine agent.

As police chief of Nashville, Truesdail's office was at 28 High Street, the former home of General Zollincoffer. He was the most powerful police figure in the city and never held his powers in restraint. I knew that Governor Johnson abhorred Truesdail from comments I heard him make at the St. Cloud during meals when the Governor sat at a nearby table. A major reason for the hostility was because Johnson had no control over Truesdail and it was useless to appeal to General Rosecrans since Rosecrans gave Truesdail free rein and never questioned his actions.

Truesdail had a position of authority which gave him respectability but underneath that veneer there was no integrity in his character. Truesdail never let ethical restraints get in the way of his side businesses of army contracts to supply beef and collect money from newspapers and magazines in order for them to circulate.

An outwardly friendly, garrulous man to those who could help him, Truesdail was a man who talked big, smiled and ingratiated himself with Union officials but was a wretched, living terror to the citizens of Nashville, all of whom he suspected of being traitors, criminals, dishonest and abhorrent. He constantly searched for spies and claimed to have agents all over Nashville, informants at hotels, the railroad station and even connected to Nashville's most prominent families. He used northern newspaper reporters who queried soldiers and then reported what they found. However, the Southern Ladies Aid Society would not be enticed by Truesdail to give up any information. Those ladies often smuggled quinine and other drugs to Rebel soldiers and, although Truesdail suspected it, he could never catch them.

From what I gathered, General Bragg wanted to draw General Rosecrans and the Union army out of Nashville for an open field battle. General Morgan and other Rebel cavalrymen were outside Nashville and Rosecrans sent troops to skirmish with them. There were regular and constant reports that Rebel troops were close to Nashville and Union troops were ordered to shoot or hang anyone who couldn't give a credible explanation of why he was where he was.

I heard from Rachel that General Morgan was headed back into Kentucky. She told me that information about the Rebel army was regularly obtained by local ladies who came to the headquarters of General Rosecrans in tears or smiles to obtain passes to visit someone, usually a sick relative, dying child or someone just outside the Federal lines.

Rachel told me that on the last day of November, General Forrest led his cavalry troops on Murfreesboro Road to within three miles of Nashville before retreating back to Murfreesboro. Everybody wondered where Bragg's army was and no one could find out. All around the city were thousands of white tents in fields and at night campfires could be seen burning for miles.

While dining one evening at the St. Cloud I overheard some young Union officers say that General Rosecrans received a telegram from Washington ordering him to drive the Rebel army across the Tennessee River as soon as possible. Great Britain's and France's decision on whether or not to support the Confederate government supposedly played a role in Washington's directive. The Union army had to control Middle Tennessee so Rosecrans set in motion plans and preparations to engage Bragg's army.

CHAPTER 49

There were slave revolts in late 1862. In Maury County, a slave burned down his master's barn after the master sold the slave's wife and child to a master in Louisiana. That slave was tracked by dogs, convicted by an on-the-spot court and hanged. A slave in Williamson County killed his master with an axe while the master slept, then appealed to Union troops for protection but that slave was also hanged.

During the early years of the War, Union troops looked at slaves as the property of their masters and the masters, in turn, warned their slaves that Union troops would torture them. Slaves as well as freed blacks were often rounded up by Union soldiers and forced to work. The slave owners felt that slavery benefitted the Negroes and insisted their slaves were loyal and happy to be slaves. The masters did not see that slavery itself was a reason for discontent amongst slaves; instead, they viewed outside agitators and the Union government waging War on them as the problem.

During the first two years of the War, neither Governor Johnson nor soldiers in the Union army believed they were fighting this War to end slavery. Governor Johnson regularly said he was fighting the slave's masters—traitorous aristocrats, he called them—and blamed them for this War.

At first, many Negroes were thrilled to see Union soldiers, which they called the "abolitionist army," come into Nashville and welcomed them with open arms. However, there were incidents of outright brutality by the Federals which led slave owners to proclaim that Negroes were much better off as slaves with loving, caring masters than free and at the mercy of whoever decided to apply physical force against them.

The Union soldiers regularly rounded up Negroes and put them to work building forts in Nashville and other labor intensive work. Slaves left plantations and flocked to the city or tagged along with soldiers as the Feds marched through the countryside. Meanwhile, planters continued to tell themselves and others how much the slaves loved them and were loyal. But the fact was that many of those loyal and loving slaves left their masters at the first opportunity and went with the Union army.

Most of the soldiers in the Union army did not want to risk their lives to free slaves; outside of the hard, manual labor the slaves did—which meant that Union soldiers avoided this labor—the slaves were mostly a nuisance that had to be fed and clothed. During the early years of the War, Union officers tended to view slaves as property belonging to their owners and so it was as some masters claimed—the slaves might attach themselves to the army but after a time they returned to their masters. However, by the end of 1862, many of the male slaves—probably most, if truth be told—had left their master's homes and farms and moved into the city of Nashville. The University of Nashville's barracks housed many of the slave refugees.

It was truly a mixed bag when it came to summing up the attitude and fate of the slaves in Nashville during the first two years of the War. Some slaves were loyal to their masters and stayed on the plantations while others either refused to work on the plantation or left to move into the city. Some slave owners tried to look out for the welfare of their slaves while others attempted to enforce discipline through beatings and violence. The slaves who left their masters were often subject to bounty hunters who ran abduction rings, capturing slaves and returning them for a price.

Some Nashvillians who fled South sent for their slaves to join them; some slaves went but others fled. There were slaves who continued to serve their masters when the owners became Confederate officers and some slaves served the Confederate army, doing a wide variety of jobs but never carrying a gun or fighting. In spite of the widely and deeply held belief amongst whites that slaves were loving and loyal to their masters and, in their heart of hearts, thankful to be slaves, almost every white Southerner was afraid that if the Negroes were armed they would become a dangerous enemy.

Newspapers reported about the lax discipline of slaves and the lack of morality in Nashville. The newspapers blamed Northerners, abolitionists and bad Negroes. The slaves who remained with their masters no longer acted like "slaves." As the War progressed it became increasingly obvious that slavery wasn't just a legal and social institution, it was a frame of mind and slaves were increasingly thinking as free people rather than as slaves.

The allegiance slaves had toward their masters and the deference shown their masters gave way to insolence and an independent spirit. Slave owners could not grasp the idea their slaves would leave plantations to live in army camps under primitive conditions or feel an allegiance to Union soldiers who often treated them meanly. Slave owners were convinced their slaves needed them but were confronted with the bitter fact that slaves did not love slavery.

This became a turning point in the War, a tipping point when slaves no longer considered themselves "slaves" so the masters could no longer be "masters." As the planters watched slaves leave plantations they abandoned the paternalistic ideals they had embraced and began to see their former slaves as problems and burdens they needed to abandon. The image of themselves as kindly slave owners was replaced by a cruelty toward their slaves as their past lives of comfort and convenience melted away. Part of it was a desperate need to survive in a new world they never expected to see.

It became a defining moment when masters realized that if slaves could walk away then they were no longer masters. The deeply held belief that slaves were happy, loyal and content was crushed and the masters' conviction that affection and allegiance bound slaves to him was proven wrong.

There were, of course, some slaves who remained with their masters, some who had genuine feelings of love and affection for their masters and who defended their masters to the point of risking their lives, but even those slaves admitted that, though they loved their masters, they did not love slavery.

CHAPTER 50

Early in the morning on the day after Christmas, 1862, I watched as General Rosecrans led his army southward. There were about 16,000 Union troops left in Nashville to defend the city. I had not heard if General Bragg planned to attack Nashville.

The next day, Rosecrans set up field headquarters eight miles outside of Nashville and sent his army towards Confederate troops, which skirmished with Rebel cavalry. On December 30, the Union army found the Confederate army waiting for them just north of Murfreesboro along Stones River, positioned on both sides of the Nashville and Chattanooga Railroad tracks. Early in the morning of New Year's Eve, we heard distant cannons and artillery in Nashville as the Battle of Stones River commenced.

On the first day of 1863, I awoke to the sound of the cannons in Murfreesboro, located about 30 miles southeast of Nashville as the Battle of Stones River took place. General Rosecrans set his army against Confederate General Bragg and, although Nashvillians thought of the dangers to their loved ones all during that day, they also felt pangs of deep joy that a battle was being fought and the Confederate army could defeat the Federals, freeing Nashville of the invaders. After a victory on the battlefield in Murfreesboro, many felt the Confederate army would march into Nashville and deliver the city out of the hands of the Northern aggressors.

In the end, nobody really won that battle; General Bragg withdrew from the field and fell back southward to Shelbyville and Tullahoma while Rosecrans held Murfreesboro. Not much news during the battle reached Nashville, which was an excruciating time for Mrs. Josiah Nichol, who had 13 grandsons in the battle. Indeed, just about every family in Nashville had at least one relative in Bragg's army.

The cost of the War came to Nashville during the next few days. By January 5, the military hospitals in Nashville were full. A number of churches—First Presbyterian Church, McKendree Methodist Church, First Baptist Church, and Cumberland Presbyterian Church—were all seized by the Union army for hospitals. It seemed like all of Nashville was one gigantic hospital.

My good friend Dr. John B. Lindsley, chancellor of the University of Nashville, relayed the horror of that battle as he worked with other surgeons on those soldiers. He told me that two Confederate Generals were killed but General Rosecrans allowed their family and friends to receive the bodies. Local Nashville women ministered to the wounded in Confederate prisons as the specter of death permeated the city. It was the first time the citizens of Nashville had been so close to a major battle.

I heard that General Braxton Bragg's troops were hungry and wore rags as they marched away from Murfreesboro. The roads were muddy, it was cold and troops foraged for whatever food they could find, tearing down wooden fences to build fires as farm families, who had been pilfered by Union troops, watched their own army empty barns and homes of food.

In Nashville, a number of physicians and nurses, sent by the Governors of Ohio, Indiana and Pennsylvania, arrived to attend to the wounded while a number of wounded were shipped to Louisville.

There was news that President Lincoln had issued an Emancipation Proclamation, effective on January 1, which freed the slaves in all of the states at War against the United States. The slaves in Tennessee were not included in this Emancipation because Governor Johnson and other Unionists in Tennessee asked Lincoln to exempt the state because Tennessee was controlled by Union forces and under the rule of a Military Governor.

The Emancipation Proclamation was controversial and caused a split between Unionists who favored abolition and those who accepted slavery but were determined to restore the Federal Union. According to Nashville courts, the existing state laws dealing with free persons of color and slaves were still in force. Negroes employed by the military were exempt from the old laws because the court could hold no jurisdiction over the army.

There was deep concern about the legal status of Negroes in Tennessee after the Emancipation. At the insistence of Governor Johnson and other local Unionist leaders, the slaves in Tennessee were still the property of their white masters although a large number of slaves had moved into the city from the outlying areas. These unwanted wards of the army lived in segregated camps.

Although soldiers in the Union army had no desire to free slaves when the War began, by the end of the second year of the War many Union soldiers felt that freeing slaves was a way of punishing the Rebels and a way to gain revenge against the Confederates for starting this War. Union commanders ordered that slaves be returned to their masters but the soldiers often ignored those orders.

CHAPTER 51

News spread in January that part of Bragg's army was headed towards Kentucky, which would put the Rebels in Nashville's rear. General Morgan's troops had been chased by Union soldiers and the Louisville and Nashville Railroad—known as the L&N—in southern Kentucky was threatened by Confederate troops while cavalry units under Wheeler and Forrest struck the Nashville and Chattanooga Railroad south of the city. The Confederate cavalry harassed steamboats on the rivers and guerillas captured and burned boats. Wheeler's cavalry burned two Louisville steamers they captured before they burned a captured gunboat. Rebels captured prisoners on a train on the Nashville and Chattanooga line, about nine miles outside of Nashville and Union officers assigned gunboats to escort steamers and barges on the Cumberland River.

The Rebel newspaper The Southern Confederacy was seen in the hands of a newsboy while a correspondent for the Chicago Tribune collected information at the St. Cloud Hotel on Midwestern troops at the Battle of Stones River; I watched the man talk with Union officers but did not speak with him myself. Copies of his report later filtered back into the city.

The Nashville area was a dangerous place as guerillas roamed the countryside and lawless bands robbed houses, stole livestock and food from farms, and terrorized local residents.

In February, Confederate units were spotted west of Nashville; indeed, it seemed like Rebel cavalry could operate freely on each side of Federal lines. As the water rose in the Cumberland, allowing boats to navigate the river, the Rebel army pestered boats south of Nashville. Rosecrans was concerned with the security of the city.

Rachel told me, as we strolled arm in arm, that General Forrest had almost been captured sometime around Christmas. She said the General had ridden out alone to check on a battle and ran right into Union soldiers, who wanted to arrest him. He asked to go back and get his troops so they could all be arrested together and they allowed him to do so; however, Forrest never had any intention of surrendering so when he got back to his troops he told them to fight their way through. He then discovered Union troops were also to his rear and he was trapped so Forrest divided his force, gave orders to charge each way, and managed to escape certain capture.

I asked if she knew about Edward and she smiled and said she'd seen him when she and her friends visited Forrest's camp and had a letter for me, which she removed from a side pocket on her dress and placed on my arm with her hand covering it. I slid my hand under hers and, after we walked a ways, placed the letter in a pocket of my coat.

Back in my room I read the letter, which said, "Dear Father, This is to let you know that I am fine. We have fought a number of small battles and General Forrest is a great General. I feel honored and lucky to ride with him. He always makes the best decisions for his troops so I am in good hands. Your loving son, Edward."

I spent the evening reading that letter over and over. It was a comfort to me.

CHAPTER 52

In the middle of February Governor Johnson left Nashville for a speaking tour of the northeast and midwest. The previous Fall the Copperhead Party, which advocated allowing the South to establish itself as a Confederacy or at least quit fighting them, won seats in the Indiana Assembly. This upset the Unionists, who were determined there would be no peace unless and until the South came back into the Union, preferably broken in spirit, contrite, and begging forgiveness for the error of her ways.

Billy brought me newspapers from different cities when he could find them and got them to me without being discovered. He brought me a paper from Indianapolis, where Governor Johnson had spoken, and the newspaper printed his remarks. The speech was a long one—Johnson was used to speaking for two or three hours at a time—and contained political oratory that sounded suspiciously like he was running for higher office.

In that speech he stated "the Government was made for the convenience of man, and not man for the Government; just as the shoe is made for the foot, not the foot for the shoe."

Johnson continued, "We have been divided into political parties—Whig and Democratic—and, latterly, Republican and Democratic. Whichever party was dissatisfied with the result of an election appealed to the people. Whatever the issue, banks or tariffs, or latterly the issues between the Democratic and Republican parties, there was waving over all the stars and stripes. All parties vied in their fealty to the Constitution and devotion to the banner of our country."

The speech continued, "Who commenced the War—this damnable struggle to destroy the people's rights? The South! Who struck the first blow, fired the first gun, shed the first blood? It is a matter of history that a delegation from Virginia urged the attack upon the Federal forts at Charleston, as a spur for Virginia to revolt."

"If I have any complaint to make, it is that President Lincoln has not done more to crush the rebellion. Has a State a right to secede? Settle the question, they say, by peaceable secession and reconstruction. This is impossible. This government cannot be divided without bloodshed. Where will you divide it? Where will you draw the line? Who shall have the territories? The framers of the Constitution designed that it should be perpetual. That instrument contains principles which are fundamental to all government, immutable, emanating from Deity himself. We are engaged in a long War, but we shall come out triumphant. Neither this nor succeeding generations shall destroy our rights."

"I hold to the theory that no State can secede. The Union was to be perpetual. Separation dissolves all bonds."

"A man builds a house in a city; it is his property and he burns it down, on the principle that he can dispose of his own property as he pleases, without regard to the rights of others, and so burns down a block, or the city. Recognize such a principle and you have no government but anarchy, and I repudiate the doctrine that a State has a right to secede, without reference to its effect on the other States. Hence I am for the Union. I intend to stand by the Union so long as I live, and shed my heart's blood, if needed, as a libation for its preservation."

"Talk about being tired of the War! I know it is terrible, and realize its horrors, but these are incidents of a Civil War. The ruin that has come, the blood that has been shed, are upon the heads of those who precipitated this Civil War, and not on ours. You who have brought on this War, have forced this ruin, set brother against brother, orphaned these children, widowed these wives, and filled the land with mourning—you have done all this—and let me ask you Rebel sympathizers to lift up your hands and see if they are not crimsoned with the blood of the victims of the rebellion? Whether it comes sooner or later, justice will come. The slower its pace, the surer is its blow. It will come, if we like; and if not living, when we are dead. Sooner or later, justice will overtake those whose hands are crimsoned with blood."

"Tired of an eighteen months' War? Your fathers fought for seven years to establish this government, and you are tired of fighting eighteen months to defend it. So far as I am concerned, I am ready to fight seven years, thirty years, and would not stop then. What is a War of thirty years, when you look at the vast results to flow from it down the sea of time, in laying the foundation of a government which will live in future ages, and revolutionize the governments of the world? Nothing! You are laying the foundation of a government which will endure while the sun rises and sets. I say, today, not from impulse, but from cool reflection, if my life was spared 700 years, I would fight on and fight ever. I would War against this Southern aristocracy as long as the Moors did against the Spaniards 700 years ago."

"Born and raised in the South, I have been a slave owner, having owned ten slaves. I obtained my Southern rights. The Rebels stole my Negroes, turned my invalid wife and children into the street, and made my house a barracks for 'Butternuts' to lie sick in. That's my Southern rights."

"I have lived among Negroes, all my life, and I am for this Government with slavery under the Constitution as it is, if the Government can be saved. I am for the Government without Negroes, and the Constitution as it is. I want to be understood on this question. I am for the government of my fathers, if it is being carried out according to the principles of the Constitution."

"If, as the State moves along, the Negroes get in the way, let them be crushed. If they keep out of the way, let them remain where they are. I am for the Government and all measures necessary to maintain it. Is not this worth more than the institution of slavery?"

"I am for the Government of my fathers with Negroes. I am for it without Negroes. Before I would see this Government destroyed I would see every Negro back in Africa, disintegrated and blotted out of space."

"If the government is to be overthrown, I do not want to survive it. If the government is to be entombed in the tomb of nation, let me be buried with it."

"Will you deny that your soldiers' blood has been shed in a glorious cause? If you do you are unworthy fathers and mothers. Who will turn his back upon his blood? (the crowd cried "traitors") Yes, traitors, none but traitors. For him who sleeps in the grave, let him know that he has fallen in a glorious cause, and water his grave with tears, and, if need be, to crown the War with success, you should shed your own blood and spend your last dollars."

CHAPTER 53

The New Nashville Theatre, the second theatre in Nashville, opened on February 24. The theatres did a lively business, presenting Shakespearean and other plays, and featured a military concert as part of each evening's show. The New Nashville Theatre was located in the Odd Fellows Building on the northwest corner of Union and Summer Streets. It was managed by Mr. Sprague, former partner in the Nashville Theatre. During the first two weeks the only entertainment that Sprague could find was minstrel music but citizens enjoyed the lighter fare.

It had been a difficult year for the theatre; from mid-January until early February the theatre was shut down because gas was shut off. It was difficult to get to the theatre during that time because streets were so muddy and sidewalks were so slippery that it was difficult to walk. On the other hand, the growing population of Nashville meant there were large crowds at both theatres when plays ran. The Nashville Theatre tended to produce classic plays while the New Nashville Theatre presented lighter fare.

Rachel and I visited the New Nashville Theatre several times during those first few weeks, although there was only minstrel music and then, at the end, a farce. The Union soldiers loved this sort of thing although Rachel and I, while we enjoyed it now and then, did not like a steady diet of it.

In May the New Nashville Theatre—which was called "Odd Fellows' Hall" until then—produced "Lucretia Borgia." This was followed by "Seven Sisters," which ran until early July. Rachel and I saw each of those plays several times and enjoyed the dramas. I also enjoyed Rachel's company; she was a lively conversationalist, although some of her views were not as well thought out as they should have been. She tended to be a bit impetuous with a tendency to fly off the handle and jump to conclusions that did not have a logical progression, but her enthusiasm was always contagious.

Rachel was emotional and passionate in her views towards the Union occupation. She resented the fact that good, upstanding loyal citizens were considered traitors and criminals. She believed she had a right to express her views without threats to her freedom and felt the police were too quick to judge and too heavy-handed in their actions against ordinary citizens. Most of all she resented the fact that day-to-day living had become so difficult in a city that was once open and free and treated visitors warmly. Citizens of Nashville had lost the privilege of being full citizens of a city where people traveled freely and expressed their views, even when they did not coincide with the views of the ruling government. Rachel liked to disagree, to argue about what was going on in life and you could not do that in a Confederate city occupied by Union forces.

When The Nashville Theatre began a series of productions Rachel and I saw the Zavistowski Troupe, a group of acrobats, and then we saw a contortionist, Signor Monteverdi, who had a week-long engagement. After that there was "The Cricket" and then "The Organ Grinder." The latter was a melodrama that made Rachel cry. It was odd to see a young woman so strong and determined melt into tears at one of those soppy dramas.

CHAPTER 54

On a Sunday in March citizens on the south side of the city were awakened by sounds of musketry and small arms fire as General Morgan fired against Federal pickets and guards on Franklin Pike. The raiders then withdrew and Morgan, disguised as a countryman, obtained a pass from a Union General—who did not know him—and went into the city where he dined at the City Hotel. After his meal, Morgan nonchalantly left the city. This was reported by the Nashville correspondent for the New York Times.

That same evening as I stood in front of the St. Cloud, I saw Rachel walking arm in arm with a Union officer. As they approached, a voice said "Good evening, Sir." It was Robert's voice! "Would you care to join us?" he asked. "Certainly," I said.

As we walked I noticed that other Union soldiers did not look at Robert; they all looked at Rachel. I commented on this and Robert said, "Of course. A young man will always look at a beautiful young lady. That's how I can walk freely in Nashville!"

Our conversation was light but Robert informed me that there were no plans to attack Nashville, despite reports to the contrary. "General Bragg wants to draw the Feds out of Nashville for a fight on open ground," he said. "However, we will continue to harass the Feds in Nashville to keep them guessing."

We walked to the Episcopal Church and sat in a pew for awhile, then Robert said, "I must be going. I have to get back with some information." Rachel smiled as she slipped some letters to Robert. Then the two arose and left the church while I stayed there a while longer.

The Union army did indeed expect an attack from Confederate forces from the South of the city; however, when this attack failed to materialize General Buell led troops to Pittsburg Landing where they joined General Grant. With Buell's departure, Governor Johnson, fearful that most of the Union troops had left the city, sent a telegram to the Secretary of War, who ordered General Halleck to take immediate measures to secure Nashville against all dangers. A Union officer told me that Governor Johnson lived in perpetual fear that Nashville would be attacked.

Those fears were not without warrant; in March a locomotive left the track after Rebels fired into the train at Lavergne and two days later a Rebel cavalry unit came within three miles of the city, capturing 500 Union prisoners, a number of Negros and horses.

Rebel attacks on the Nashville and Chattanooga Railroad continued. In April, Rebels attacked a passenger train four miles north of Lavergne and derailed the train. Rebels set the cars and locomotive on fire and reports indicated 75-80 were killed while over one hundred Union soldiers were taken prisoner. General Wheeler led an artillery assault as a train crossed a river nine miles northeast of Nashville. The Confederate soldiers, hidden behind trees, opened fire on the steam locomotive with 18 cars and ruptured the boiler, which stopped the train. The Rebels destroyed the locomotive and during the fight most of the horses were killed, which was the principle cargo.

Fearing an attack on Nashville in April, General Rosecrans issued orders to prepare for a surprise attack. Nashville's streets were barricaded and troops were in defensive positions; a requisition for 4,000 horses was issued but horses were hard to find so citizens found their horses unhooked from buggies and wagons and seized by Union soldiers.

That day the distant sounds of heavy cannon fire were heard, which caused great excitement in Nashville. Negroes were impressed to reinforce fortifications and there was panic among businessmen as Union officers rounded up horses indiscriminately while citizens crowded the post commander's office seeking return of their horses.

There were announcements in the newspapers that claimed an "unprecedented crisis" in May as many citizens reluctantly took the Loyalty Oath; however, many others fled south. The women of Nashville remained the staunchest of Rebel supporters despite threats, oaths and paroles.

In May, Confederate cavalry units conducted raids within eight miles of downtown Nashville and captured several Union pickets. A few days later there were more raids north of Nashville in Goodlettsville.

CHAPTER 55

On a beautiful day in May, Rachel was nearly breathless when she came to my room. "Have you heard about Captain Van Dorn?" she asked.

"No, I replied—what happened."

"Dr. Peters killed him yesterday."

Dr. George Peters, a respected medical doctor, lived at Rippaville, a plantation about 30 miles southwest of Nashville.

"Van Dorn was having an affair with Dr. Peters' wife, Jessie," said Rachel. "Or at least he had given her a lot of attention—I don't know exactly. But Captain Van Dorn has always been known as a ladies man and it seems that he loved one lady that he shouldn't have."

Earl Van Dorn was certainly known in Nashville. He came from Mississippi and was the great nephew of Andrew Jackson, which was as close to royalty as you could get in Tennessee. Van Dorn, like Forrest, led a cavalry unit. Van Dorn was a West Point graduate who had a thirst for glory and distinction, which led him to engage in some risky ventures. At the Elkhorn Tavern in Arkansas he had been defeated and suffered another defeat in Corinth after Shiloh. That led to accusations that he was drunk during a battle and paid more attention to the ladies than to his troops. A court of inquiry cleared him but the gossip always flowed freely around Van Dorn.

There was something about Van Dorn that attracted women. He was dashing and charming, which must have made up for the fact that he was only five feet five inches tall. He had a dark complexion and a big shaggy mustache, which must have tickled the ladies in various places.

"Jessie Peters was Dr. Peters' third wife," said Rachel. "And she was a lot younger than him. Twenty-four years. They were married because of politics and to keep that plantation."

I had heard something along those lines.

"One of my friends said Captain Van Dorn was known as 'the terror of ugly husbands' because he had seduced so many wives."

I had heard rumors to that affect as well.

"Van Dorn was sitting at a desk in Ferguson Hall," said Rachel. "That's owned by Martin Cheairs, you know."

Yes, I knew that.

"That was his headquarters and he was writing when Dr. Peters walked up behind him and shot him in the back of his head." She paused and we looked at each other silently. "He died a couple of hours later and Dr. Peters left in a buggy, headed south."

I knew this was a tragedy for all those involved, but my regret that Captain Earl Van Dorn was dead was because he and General Forrest were excellent cavalry leaders who made the Union army in Nashville nervous. The Rebels could not spare any officer who might help liberate Nashville.

CHAPTER 56

During the first half of 1863 the Emancipation Proclamation led to speeches, discussions of the edict and expressions of concern for the future of Negroes. Bounty hunters continually sought slaves, ostensibly to return them to owners but in reality to smuggle them south for rewards offered by the Confederate government and army. Slaves who fled their Rebel masters for protection from the Union army were exempt from arrest as fugitives and the Provost Marshal enforced this special privilege. The presence of contrabands caused housing problems. During the first week in April, 50 wagon loads of contrabands of all ages arrived in the city from the lower counties.

The army detective police, commanded by Colonel Truesdail, engaged in ruthless behavior against citizens all during the first half of 1863. There were several layers of armed officials patrolling Nashville, enforcing laws, making arrests and badgering citizens but Truesdail was the most tyrannical.

Truesdail employed a large number of spies in Nashville, separate from Grenville M. Dodge, head of an intelligence gathering organization for the Union army set up by General Grant, which also had spies in Nashville.

Actress Pauline Cushman, who appeared in the Nashville Theatre's production of "The Married Rake" in spring, 1863, was a dedicated Union spy, although she was outspokenly pro-southern. The beautiful actress, along with several other Rebel women, was "expelled" from the city by Truesdail in late May. Coached by Truesdail, she entered the camps of General Bragg in and around Shelbyvile and Columbia and captured maps from a table used by Confederate commanders.

In April, Fannie Battle, daughter of Confederate General Joel Battle, and Harriet Booker were arrested by Union authorities and charged with being spies and smugglers and forging passes. They were arrested as they left town to cross into Rebel lines, carrying a large quantity of letters and messages for Confederates. They were sent to Camp Chase and described by Union officers as "incorrigible."

That was the beginning of a number of arrests in Nashville in mid-April; soon, every man on the street without a pass was arrested and at night, citizens often heard a knock on their door and were taken away.

David Lipscomb, a devoted pacifist, argued the cause of conscientious objectors until Governor Johnson reportedly assured him that he and others who held that position would not be forced into military service. In addition to Lipscomb, there were several other pacifists and conscientious objectors.

Nashville merchant Jacob Bloomstein was arrested by Truesdail and charged with smuggling supplies to the Rebels. After his arrest, Bloomstein's store lost $6,000 worth of merchandise, taken by unknown persons with no interference from the police. Bloomstein accused Truesdail of involvement in the heist. Truesdail did conduct "personal business" in this manner as well as profit from a contract that allowed him to carry the mail to soldiers in the Department of the Cumberland. General Rosecrans, who protected Truesdail against the complaints of Governor Johnson and numerous citizens, supplied

Truesdail with horses and wagons as well as five soldiers to help deliver the mail. Since he controlled the mails, Truesdail became the agent for the delivery of newspapers to soldiers. Truesdail controlled the circulation of the newspapers so none were delivered until the publishers made financial arrangements with him. Additionally, Truesdail also speculated in cotton and often used General Rosecrans' name in order to obtain favorable prices and conditions for sales.

CHAPTER 57

On the evening of May 30, Governor Johnson, with his wife Eliza, daughter Mary Stover and her children and William Browning returned to Nashville. Johnson had been to Washington, then to Louisville where he met his wife and they stayed a few days—she was not well—before coming to Nashville.

A large group of citizens met the Governor and his family at the depot and a brass band welcomed them with songs. Accompanied by a group of infantry and a group of cavalry, the Governor and his entourage climbed into two carriages and rode up College and Cedar streets to his house. It was quite an event; the band played "Hail Columbia" and citizens cheered the Governor. When the party arrived at their house, the crowd yelled for a speech.

Governor Johnson said he did not have a speech to give at that time but wanted to sincerely thank the citizens and soldiers for the heart-warming reception they had been given. He reported what he said over a year ago when he came, that he "returned to them with the olive branch of peace, the Constitution, and the laws."

"There can be no peace, except by obedience to the Constitution and the Laws," Johnson told the crowd. "You have prospered and been happy under the Constitution and the Laws of your country, you ought to submit now, and be happy once more." Members of the crowd yelled "God bless you, Governor Johnson!" while other voices said "Amen!" and another voice proclaimed "Good."

"I am come to ameliorate the condition of my fellow-citizens," said Johnson as cheers erupted from the crowd. "I have a responsible duty to perform to you, and to my country, and God willing, that duty will be faithfully performed, as far as my humble ability extends. Did I ever deceive you?"

Voices in the crowd answered "Never, Never."

"Never," repeated Johnson, "nor do I wish or intend to do so now. I wish to retain that confidence. Shall I have it?"

Voices from the crowd proclaimed "Yes! you shall!"

"I will not flatter you," said Johnson. "I will not deceive you. This is my adopted State; in it are all that I hold dearly. Here are my wife and family, my property, my all; and I desire to free the State from treason and rebellion. Be true to yourselves, to your country, and to her laws, and all will be well."

CHAPTER 58

In June, the citizens of Nashville believed the Rebel army would attack the city at the end of the month; late in the month there was indeed a Rebel raid on the Nashville and Chattanooga railroad between Nashville and Murfreesboro and a few days later the Rebels skirmished with Union army railroad guards north of Nashville in Sumner County.

On the Fourth of July an official celebration was held at Fort Gillem on Harden's Hill, a mile west of the Capitol. The city shook as 35 guns were fired. Church bells pealed, bands played, a parade was held, and a brigade of Negro soldiers along with two or three other regiments marched. Parson Brownlow and Governor Johnson spoke at the Capitol. Celebrations were also held in Edgefield, at Berry's Grove on Franklin Pike and on Jefferson Street.

Earlier that month, the Union army began enlisting Negro recruits in Gallatin to fight the Rebels. This was an affront to white Southerners who believed that Negro troops fighting Rebels was unthinkable. It was a hard, deep blow against Southern sympathizers when they saw a Negro in a Union military uniform carrying a rifle.

A few days after the July Fourth celebration Rachel saw me as I entered the dining room at St. Cloud and whispered "leave your door unlocked this evening." A little before 11 that night, as I sat in my chair reading, I heard the door knob turn and Edward entered quickly. "I need a place to sleep," he said. I offered my bed but he said, “No, no—I just want some space on the floor” and then added, “If I sleep in a bed I’ll become spoiled. Besides, I wouldn’t get a good night’s sleep—a bed is foreign to me.” He said this with a smile.

We had to keep our voices low and Edward spoke in almost a whisper. He told me that Confederates in the fort at Vicksburg had surrendered to General Grant and that General Robert E. Lee’s Rebel troops had been beaten in a battle in Pennsylvania. We knew the Confederate defenders in Vicksburg could not hold out much longer—they had been under siege for eight months. I had also heard that General Lee and his army had left Virginia and headed North.

Edward told me that General Bragg had moved his army further east, over the Cumberland Mountains and there were Confederate troops in the southern part of Middle Tennessee which the Union army planned to drive out of the state. The problem the Union army faced was hit and run attacks by guerrilla forces and Southern cavalry, especially those led by Generals Morgan, Wheeler and Forrest.

I asked Edward if he had heard from his brother and he took a letter out of his pocket. Robert wrote “This is to let you know that I am well and we are having success against the enemy. General Morgan likes to surprise them and he does that well. We talk often about Nashville but we must take each day as it comes. I hope you are well and that I will see you soon, although I don’t know when that will be. It is a hard life but I remind myself that we are fighting a noble fight for a noble cause and hope that justice will prevail. Please send a letter by the carrier if you can.” Robert signed it “your loving son, Robert.”

“Can you get a letter to him?” I asked Edward. He nodded. After Edward was asleep I took out pen and paper and wrote, “Dear Robert.

It was good to hear from you and know you're well. I treasure every word I receive from you. We remain optimistic that things will turn out well and know you serve honorably." I spoke about the weather, that I lived comfortably at the hotel and that I saw Matthew from time to time but we did not talk much.

It seemed like the tide was turning against the Confederacy in the summer of 1863. The defeats in Vicksburg and Pennsylvania indicated turning points in the War but many Southern loyalists in Nashville clung to the belief that the Rebels would rally and, further, Nashville would be liberated, although it was hard to sustain optimism in the light of those recent events and because the Union army seemed to be in full control of Nashville. That hit home when the street barricades were removed in August, which indicated the Union army felt no threat from Confederate forces.

The biggest setback for Union soldiers came when all the white prostitutes were sent out of the city to Louisville—the black prostitutes were exempted from this action—but they didn't stay exiled in Kentucky for long. Early the next month, most of the prostitutes returned and there were whispers that one prostitute had disguised herself as a Union soldier and circulated amongst the troops until her disguise was uncovered. The problem with sending prostitutes out of Nashville was that no other city would accept them. In mid-August those prostitutes were back in Nashville but were required to be inspected by army surgeons because venereal disease was running rampant. From that point forward the prostitutes were required to carry a certificate, signed by a medical officer stating they did not have any venereal disease. They were free to continue to ply their trade as long as they were examined every two weeks.

CHAPTER 59

August proved to be an interesting month. William G. Harding paid a visit to Governor Andrew Johnson. Harding began the conversation by asking about the enlistment of Negroes in Tennessee. Harding told the Governor, "I have a daughter now in the North, and if it is the intention of the Federal authorities to employ Negro soldiers, I shall let her remain there, rather than bring her back to a State which will become the theatre of indiscriminate violence, robbery, rape, bloodshed and every species of outrage perpetrated by Negro soldiers, who will have no regard for the lives, and property of citizens, or the chastity of women." Harding was speaking of his daughter, Selene Harding, who was enrolled in Madame Masse's private French school in Philadelphia.

The Governor countered, "Before you inveigh against the policy of the Federal Government, which you claim the privilege of criticizing, you ought to ask yourself, who brought this state of things upon the country and who was responsible for it? You talk of outrages and the violation of female chastity, when your Confederate Government has Indian savages employed in hunting Tennessee loyalists to their hiding places in the mountains, and when your Rebel cavalrymen are now engaged in seizing and stripping women in the mountains, under pretext of ascertaining whether they are men disguised in female garments to escape Conscription. These brutalities are perpetrated daily by your friends and you are silent."

Harding replied, "But Governor, I do not approve of these things at all; I am opposed to them."

The Governor angrily replied, "Of course you are opposed to them now; because you dare not express yourself otherwise. But you helped to set on foot the rebellion, which is the parent of all these crimes and sufferings. You boasted that you had circulated five million dollars to promote the rebellion, in the once quiet and happy state of Tennessee. Sir, if I had done what you have done, my hands and every thread of my garments would seem to blush with the blood of my murdered countrymen. You are responsible for the murder of the flower of the youth of Tennessee, and the desolation of her households. You are one of the conspirators who delivered them over to an untimely and ignominious death, in battle against their country, in order that you might hold to your Negro property. You and your guilty comrades are red and dripping with the blood of your deluded victims."

Harding had indeed been a member of Tennessee's three-man military and financial board which by October, 1861, had spent over $4.6 million to arm the state and stated they intended to spend over $5 million. Harding had been brigadier general in the state militia under Johnson prior to the Civil War and was nominated by Johnson in 1856 as a penitentiary inspector but was not confirmed.

Harding answered, "I obeyed the dictates of my conscience in all that I did, as I did when I held office under you, in years past. Did you not once consider me worthy of trust?"

"Yes, I did," said Johnson. "Once you were considered an honorable man. But Benedict Arnold was once a faithful soldier, and fought bravely for his country, then he turned traitor and endeavored to sell her to the enemy and he died in disgrace. Aaron Burr was also once deemed an honorable man and a brave soldier, but he too died a universally detested traitor."

"Do you compare me to Arnold and Burr?" asked Harding.

"Yes," replied Johnson. "I consider you a traitor, an enemy of your country. If you regret your misconduct why do you not make amends for it by openly espousing the cause of the country against the rebellion, instead of carping at and censuring the policy of the Government?"

"I am under bonds at present," said Harding.

"And why are you under bonds?" asked Johnson, "except that you are an unrepentant enemy of your State and country. You have stirred up mutiny, insurrection, and anarchy in this State, and instead of helping us put the rebellion down, you are here denouncing the inhumanity and brutality of the Federal Government and the barbarism of the Northern people, at the very same time you are keeping your own daughter among these very Northern people for quiet and protection! Be assured, sir, that the Government is determined to put down this rebellion in any way, and by any means it may choose to select, without regard to the fault-finding and objections of Rebels and malcontents. And it is equally determined to bring all traitors to a strict and terrible accountability. Wealth and position shall not shield a traitor from the avenging justice of the people."

Word of that encounter spread rapidly and was even reported in the Union newspaper.

CHAPTER 60

Little Billy came up to me on the street and said, "City Hotel at noon."

As soon as I walked in the door of the hotel a young lady came up to me and said, "Your room is ready. I'll show you to it." I followed her upstairs and she unlocked a room. I stepped in and saw Robert with three other young men.

"We had quite a wild ride," he said. "We were gone for awhile." The other young men smiled.

I looked around the room and said, "It's good to see you, Robert."

"It's good to see you, too," said Robert. "General Morgan had us ride through Kentucky and then into Indiana and Ohio, almost all the way to Pennsylvania."

"That's quite a ride," I said.

"Yeah, we spent 21 hours straight in the saddle one day, trying to avoid Union cavalry. We spent 18 to 20 hours straight in the saddle on other days. Got in a big fight and lost about 800 men. We were caught beside the Ohio River and most got captured, including General Morgan, but we managed to escape."

"Where's he now?" I asked.

"In the Ohio State Penitentiary."

"Sounds serious," I said. "How did you make it back?"

"Hard riding, a little lying and some luck."

I just stood and looked at him, thankful he was safe.

"I never want to put you in a position where you are in danger," said Robert. "But we have to have some things delivered to some friends."

"What is it?" I asked.

Robert pulled out a box from under the bed; in it were four pistols, several rounds of ammunition and a package wrapped in brown paper. It looked like a book. I stood there wondering how I was going to get all of those pistols and ammunition out of there when a key turned in the doorway. Robert shoved the box back under the bed as everyone froze. Rachel walked in and said, "I'm sorry I couldn't come sooner. I came as soon as I got your message."

I turned to Rachel and said, "We've got to get some things out of here."

"I know," said Rachel. "Where are they?"

Robert pulled the box from under the bed and Rachel picked up the pistols. "I will face the wall but you gentlemen must turn your heads."

Rachel had thin ropes tied to her hoop under her skirt and she tied the pistols to those ropes. She took the ammunition and put it in a pouch hanging from those ropes. "You'll have to take that package," she said.

Mrs. Monahan had sewn a large pocket on the inside back of my coat. I had never used it until now but I put the package in that pocket and it fit perfectly.

"That package has to go to Billy," she said. "I'll take care of the rest."

I shook hands with Robert and left. Outside the hotel I saw Billy and said, "I need to see you." He nodded and I walked several blocks before I went to the Episcopal Church. Billy was waiting for me inside; I went into a pew and knelt as if I was praying. Billy stayed in the back. I stayed in the praying position, waiting for Billy, then turned around to see where he was. Three policemen were standing behind me.

"It's an odd time to be praying," said one. "I never knew you were a praying man."

"In times like these everyone needs to pray," I answered. "We need all the Divine help we can get."

"Who are you?" another asked.

"Walter Duncan. I live at the St. Cloud Hotel. Governor Johnson and a number of officers have seen me there." I paused and then said, "I've signed the Loyalty Oath."

"And you've abided by it?" asked the first policeman.

"To the best of my ability," I replied.

"Yes, I know who he is," said the policeman who had not spoken. "I've seen him dining with officers."

The three policemen looked at each other, stepped back a few steps and whispered amongst themselves, then looked at me hard. "We should take him in," one said.

That's when Billy came up to me and said, "You promised you would help my Mom."

"Yes, I did," I said. "Is she not well?"

The first policemen then said, "We saw you come out of the City Hotel and wondered why you'd be there with the secesh crowd."

"I dine there from time to time," I replied. "I like to have a little variety in my diet."

The policemen continued to stand there. "Tell your Mom I'll help her as soon as I can," I said to Billy.

"But we know your sons are secesh. Have you seen them lately?"

"Do you mean Matthew, who works at the telegraph office?" I asked.

A surprised look came on their faces. "Is Matthew your son?" one asked.

"Yes," I said, "Matthew Duncan. He works at the telegraph office."

"I had breakfast with him this morning," one said. He paused and then turned, "Let's go," he said to the others and they walked out of the church.

I stood up, took Billy's hand and we walked outside. "I need to go to my room," I said.

Billy and I walked several blocks, circling the St. Cloud, then he left and I went back to my room. Just before I went to dinner, a knock came on the door. "Come in." It was Billy.

Without a word, I handed him the package from the back of my coat and he left.

CHAPTER 61

On a Saturday at the end of August there was a meeting of Unionists at the Courthouse in Franklin, about 20 miles south of Nashville. The purpose of the meeting was to devise a way to reorganize the State government so it would again be part of the Union. The Courthouse was full of Unionists who enjoyed a fiery speech by Parson Brownlow before Governor Johnson arrived by special train. A few days later, Matthew came by the hotel while I sat in the lobby and gave me a newspaper that had a text of that speech. "I thought you might want to see this," said Matthew. I thanked him and asked how he was doing; "Well," he replied, "and you?"

"It is a difficult time," I said. "I wish things were as they used to be." Matthew looked away before he looked back at me and said, "I know how you feel, Father, but we both know that can never be."

"I know, son," I replied. "But a man can always hope."

Matthew turned away and I asked, "Were you at the meeting in Franklin?"

"Yes, I was," he said. "I, ah, ah" and his voice trailed off. Then he said, "I heard you saw some of my friends recently."

"Yes," I said. "We had a conversation. They seemed to be gentlemen."

Matthew smiled when I said that and then bid me farewell. He did not ask about his brothers.

The newspaper reported Johnson's long speech; it did not contain any great surprises.

In the speech, Johnson stated "The States were to be united forever. The idea of unity and freedom was a Divine one, recorded in the beginning, and the Government was to be perpetual." He asserted that "This is not a War of the North against the South, nor of the South against the North. It is a wicked rebellion on the one hand, and a just and constitutional War for its suppression on the other. The Government is suppressing a rebellion—an injunction of our fathers, as written in the Constitution."

Most of the speech was vintage Johnson, who declared "I deny the doctrine of secession wholly, absolutely, in total. Tennessee is not out of the Union, never has been and never will be out. The bonds of the Constitution and the Federal power will always prevent that. This government is perpetual; provision is made for reforming the Government, amending the Constitution, and admitting States into the Union, not for letting them out of it."

"Many humble men," said Johnson, "the peasantry and yeomanry of the South, who have been decoyed, or perhaps driven into the rebellion, may look forward with reasonable hope, for an amnesty. But the intelligent and influential leaders must suffer. The tall poppies must be struck down."

Ah, the tall poppies must be struck down. That's what Johnson intends to do after this War ends. It will not end in a negotiated peace, if Johnson has his way. The Governor attacked the idea of a compromise, stating, "After wading in blood and carnage, and filling the land with desolation, these Rebels when whipped turn about and talk of a compromise! I have no compromise to offer, save the

Constitution and the laws. Obey these and the difficulty will be settled in forty-eight hours."

Johnson wanted to calm the white population, who feared a country where slaves are free. He asserted, "I believe the white basis of representation to be most just and most in accordance with the spirit of our institutions. I am for a white man's government, and for a free, intelligent, white constituency, instead of a Negro aristocracy."

"The time once was when we could discuss all questions, political or theological, except slavery," continued Johnson. "Fellow-citizens, whenever you cannot discuss any institution of a State, then liberty is gone. You said slavery was above the Government, and in seeking to confirm this your plot recoiled. If in this recoil slavery must go, I say, let it go! I am for my Government with or without slavery; but if either the Government or slavery must perish, I say give me the Government and let the Negroes go. I believe if they do go, that in less than ten years they will be more productive than they are now."

"Cotton and Negroes have ruled here in the South; they are rulers no longer. The world got along very well for four thousand years without being aware of the existence of King Cotton. It has been in general use for some ninety years, and some people think that without it the sun would cease rising and the world would be ruined. A little more silk, flax, and wool will displace it effectually. The government is above cotton and Negroes. Rather than have it destroyed I would send every Negro back to Africa."

Johnson concluded his speech saying, "Let me say to the ladies in no unkind spirit, the female sex have done much to get up this rebellion. We know how very much you can do now to restore prosperity and happiness. Help to chase away this malignant planet of fire and blood which is now in the ascendant. There is a power behind the throne. Set about to work for your country, as patriot women did in olden time."

There was music from brass bands and other speakers followed and the Unionists felt their cause was just and would triumph.

CHAPTER 62

Rachel and I were walking when we saw a large crowd approaching. They were Unionists who had held a rally at the Capitol building and were now parading through the streets. They were headed for Governor Johnson's house so we followed. The crowd called on him for a speech and he finally came out of his house and spent the next two hours in an impromptu talk. What he said during that speech was quite surprising and unusual for him; it was certainly a shock to hear his new message.

Johnson proclaimed, "The system of Negro slavery has proved baleful to the nation by arraying itself against the institutions and interests of the people, and the time has clearly come when means should be devised for its total eradication from Tennessee."

"Slavery was a cancer on our society and the scalpel of the statesman should be used not simply to pare away the exterior and leave the roots to propogate the disease anew, but to remove it altogether," continued Johnson. "Let us destroy the cause of our domestic dissensions and this bloody Civil War. It is neither wise nor just to compromise with an evil so gigantic."

I had never heard—or heard of—Johnson setting himself unequivocally against slavery. In this speech he wanted it removed, either immediately or gradually, because he believed slavery was a curse and needed to be extinguished without delay. Governor

Johnson had to swallow his pride to make that speech, supporting the emancipation of all Negros. It was a difficult speech for him to give because it was a reversal of his earlier beliefs.

CHAPTER 63

At the beginning of September Jacob Bloomstein was released from prison and returned to Nashville, where he discovered that Truesdail's men had emptied his store of all his goods and merchandise, including 3,000 pounds of cotton. Further, they had destroyed all his records so he could not make any claims for theft and damage.

By mid-September Nashville had changed because of the construction of defensive works. The fortification of the State Capitol, which was protected by earthworks and a palisade of cedar logs and defended by fourteen guns made it an imposing target. Fort Negley, which had 112 heavy guns, sent a clear message to the citizens of Nashville who sympathized with the South. However, Rachel told me the guns were usually undermanned and there was not much ammunition available.

Toward the end of September, the first wounded from the Battle of Chickamauga arrived in Nashville on the Nashville and Chattanooga Railroad. The following day, citizens in Nashville received word that a number of Rebel soldiers from Davidson County, under the commands of General Frank Cheatham and General George Maney, had been killed in that battle. I could not stop thinking of Edward, but I heard no reports of any of General Forrest's troops being victims in that battle.

Within a few days, prisoners of War from the battle began to reach Nashville to the point where over a thousand Confederate prisoners of War were in the city. The prisoners were marched to the Public Square, then to the Capitol where they answered a roll call and then dispatched to their places of detention.

After the Battle of Chickamauga, General Grant relieved Rosecrans of command of the Army of Tennessee, which meant that Truesdail lost his protector. The Daily Union fired a series of volleys at Truesdail; the editor accused him of blackmail because he refused to circulate that paper through his agency, which was the sole distributor of newspapers and magazines to 60,000 Union soldiers. According to the editor, Truesdail only wanted popular articles about himself in the paper. Truesdail was also accused of seizing and selling Rebel property at will with no accounting.

Actually, Truesdail wasn't trusted by Governor Johnson, who described him as a man "wholly incompetent, if not corrupt, in the grossest sense of the term." His reign of terror lasted for a year; during that time he abused his power to arrest and jail citizens and enriched himself by confiscating cotton and then claiming to sell it on behalf of the Union army while pocketing the profits. However, when Truesdail claimed to issue orders under the authority of General Rosecrans, he was called down; General Rosecrans had given no such orders.

CHAPTER 64

Little Billy ran up to me as I walked down Cherry Street, cocked his finger at me so that I bent down, and whispered "City Hotel at seven" and then ran off. A few minutes before seven that evening I went into the City Hotel and was met by the owner, Mrs. Mary Winburn, who led me to the back where she opened a door that led to the basement. The room was dark with only a few candles burning. I stood there, letting my sight adjust, and saw Robert there with four or five other men; they all appeared a bit nervous. I did not say anything, only nodded, and then the door opened again and Rachel entered.

Everyone was subdued but Rachel told an amusing story of Captain Frank Battle, a member of General Wheeler's cavalry, who dressed like a woman and passed through Union lines. He wanted to obtain copies of the local newspapers and, after he did so, returned back to Confederate headquarters in Tullahoma.

Robert said, "I have something for you" and handed me two letters. "You should read them later," he said, and then told me about a military order from Union officials in Nashville that demanded all citizens with southern sympathies leave the city. He then related the story of Private Sam Davis.

A month or two previous, Private Davis, a 21-year-old native of Rutherford County, just south of Nashville, and an experienced Southern scout, entered Nashville after the Battle of Chickamauga to ascertain the strength of the Federal military units between Nashville and Decatur, Alabama in order to provide General Bragg with information on Federal plans.

Just outside Nashville, Davis met with two other scouts—James Castleman and P.N. Matlock—who were also collecting information for Bragg. They came into the city dressed as civilians and checked into the St. Cloud Hotel. At the St. Cloud they dined one night with three Union Generals and engaged in a spirited discussion of the tactics of both armies at Chickamauga.

I remembered those young men and passed along several papers I received from Rachel to them. I had also taken several papers from them and given them to Rachel. I had not looked at those papers; I was told to not do so and do not know what they contained.

According to Robert, the three Rebel spies stayed for two weeks and during that time secured maps, descriptions of local fortifications and reported on the strength of the Union army in Tennessee. They also arranged with a Nashville citizen to purchase Federal side arms, which were stored in an outbuilding near his home. The trio were to pick up the weapons as they left the city. Robert did not say whether he or his group had anything to do with those weapons, but I don't believe he would have told me if they were innocent of that activity.

On November 19, Davis, Castleman and Matlock found three horses tied at the courthouse. The horses belonged to Union officers who left pistols strapped to each horse. The three rode south out of town and picked up the 47 pistols hidden for them.

Davis, who carried maps and papers, took eight pistols and split from the other two. The next day he was arrested by Federal scouts who put him in jail in Pulaski and charged him with spying because of the maps and papers. General Grenville Dodge questioned him, as did other Union officials, but Davis refused to divulge his sources or his comrades.

A military trial was held on November 23 and Davis was found guilty and ordered to be hanged. The Southern spy chose to become a martyr; he refused to reveal his sources or his friends before he was hanged four days later in Pulaski by Union troops. "We must be careful," said Robert. "I do not want you in harm's way, but thought you should know this." I nodded. He said, "We must go" and left.

I walked to the St. Cloud in a round-about way and did not take out the letters until I got to my room. I recognized the handwriting on the first envelope; it was from my sister-in-law in Atlanta. "Dear Walter," it said. "This is a horrible War and I wish it would soon be over. There is so much trouble here, although it is not as bad as Nashville where you have the Union army everywhere. My husband doesn't know how he will get his cotton crop in. There have been soldiers from both armies who have stolen our food, animals and terrorized us, although, thank goodness, we have not been harmed. There are armed bands of men terrorizing everyone. But there is also good news here—I am going to be a Grandmother! The doctor said that we should expect the arrival in late Spring or early Summer. The doctor picked the date June 1. I hope you are doing well. I have received no letters from Robert, Edward or Matthew and hope each is doing well. I have heard the news about Matthew and can't believe he has done that to this family. I pray I can forgive him when this War is over. I miss my dear sister who was your loving wife. I hope you are doing well. Yours, Elizabeth."

The second letter was from Edward, who wrote "Dear Father, Times are hard here. We don't get much to eat and we're always short of everything. Still, we persist because our cause is just. We have to sleep back to back on cold nights. I have shoes but the soles are thin. I am lucky because many do not. If you find coats and blankets please save them. Your loving son, Edward."

CHAPTER 65

At the end of November, Generals Grant, Sherman, Gordon Granger, Philip Sheridan, John A. Logan and Grenville Dodge were in Nashville. The Generals first met with Governor Johnson and that evening went to the theatre where they saw "Hamlet." General Sherman, who loved the theatre, disliked the performance of "Hamlet" and began to openly criticize from the audience, claiming the actors were "murdering" the play.

General Sherman may have taken to heart the lines by Polonius in the first act, "This above all—to thine own self be true; And it must follow, as the night the day, Thou canst not then be false to any man" because the volatile Sherman was certainly being true to himself that evening. The lines from Hamlet, "The time is out of joint; O cursed spite, That ever I was born to set it right" may also have struck home with the General.

Although Sherman was upset with the performance, General Dodge quieted him before many noticed his comments. Interestingly, none of the Generals were recognized by the citizens or soldiers who attended the play that evening.

During the Christmas season Generals Dodge and Sherman dined at the residence of post commander General Robert Granger. Granger's mother proved to be a difficult dinner companion, criticizing Dodge for allowing himself to live off the country and criticized Sherman for sweeping the country between Chattanooga and Nashville so clean that citizens were left with no shoes, clothing or food.

"The old army never would have committed such acts," she said. Sherman accepted full responsibility and countered that he always stood up for his soldiers and he ordered them to fend for themselves because no provision had been made. He told her the people who were allegedly plundered "were doing nothing for their country and deserved little pity."

On Christmas night, General Grant left Nashville for Knoxville; that month, a large number of prisoners of War came into the city. Also, General Granger ordered all powder removed to locations outside the city because citizens were afraid of a thunderstorm when so many powder magazines were in the city.

CHAPTER 66

On the first day of 1864 the temperature was zero. A number of Negroes decided to hold a parade in honor of the first anniversary of The Emancipation Proclamation, which was a little odd considering that Tennessee was not included. Only about 50 showed up and they marched behind a bass drum pounding away.

By this time slaves could be freed just by walking away from their masters and going to a contraband camp—which were ghettos full of graft—or by joining the Union army. There were a number of public jobs that employed Negroes and many of those employed still lived and ate at their master's. Authorities considered them to still be slaves if they stayed with their masters.

On that first day of the year, actor Edwin Adams presented a Shakespeare play; Rachel and I saw him perform in both "Hamlet" and "Macbeth." But the real treasure came when John Wilkes Booth was engaged for two weeks at the beginning of February. His brother, Edwin Booth, was considered to be the best actor in America but Rachel and I felt that John Wilkes Booth was his equal. We saw him perform "Richard III," a classic Shakespeare play.

"Now is the winter of our discontent" from the lips of Richard III was a perfect description of Nashville and when Richard, Duke of Gloucester said "But then I sigh, and, with a piece of scripture, Tell them that God bids us do good for evil: And thus I clothe my naked villainy, With odd old ends, stol'n out of holy writ; And seem a saint, when most I play the devil" was a perfect description of some of Nashville's clergy.

The play is about intrigue and War and I shuddered when I heard the lines from Richard III, "Conscience is but a word that cowards use, Devis'd at first to keep the strong in awe; Our strong arms be our conscience, swords our law." There was no better way to describe Governor Johnson and the Union army during that War in Nashville.

CHAPTER 67

The countryside surrounding Nashville was a lawless no-man's land by 1864. Citizens cheered the guerillas when they disrupted a Union train or boat or when they ambushed Union soldiers, but those same guerillas could also be lawless bandits who robbed locals of food and held summary executions for those who were suspected of harboring Union sympathies. Sometimes the guerillas were wrong in their accusations but men pay with their lives when this type of justice is meted out. I hoped Robert remained safe.

The guerillas were guided by political and social ideals but the bandits had no political philosophy they defended; they lived to rob and steal. It was difficult for rural citizens during this time; desperate people do desperate things and hunger creates a desperation which can lead to lawlessness.

By 1864 it was becoming obvious that not only could the South lose the War, they could also lose a way of life and a society that had been built up over two centuries. There was an ideology that was being dismantled which whites in particular did not want to relinquish. Still, morale remained high the South would persevere and would win this War, not by military victory but by sheer perseverance. Southerners knew that most of those in the North would just as soon let them go.

Emotions would rise and fall, depending on battlefield victories or defeats but there remained a deep, underlying, undying belief that the South was right and would prevail if only they could hold on until the other side simply quit fighting and went back home so this War would not have been in vain.

The thing that kept Southern sympathizers smiling during this period was the guerilla raids on the railroads and ships bringing in troops and supplies. There were daily reports of robberies, burglaries and thievery; the police had little success in solving crimes or stopping the violence.

Since civilians were forbidden to have arms, they could not protect themselves against bands of robbers. In April there were a number of highway robberies; a few days later a gang of 12 boys, ages eight to sixteen, were arrested for burglaries and theft. There were also robberies by men dressed in a Federal soldier's uniforms.

During May, there were reports of guerillas all around Nashville; a plain clothes highwayman robbed four men near Brentwood, just south of Nashville, and killed one who resisted. Guerillas in Williamson County were reported harassing citizens loyal to the Union and the next day over a hundred Rebel guerillas drove off Union soldiers around Fort Donelson.

In June there was increased guerrilla activity along the Cumberland River below the city. Mounted guerillas tore up a section of the track between Cowan and Decherd and some of Forrest's cavalry—reports indicated 150-200 troops—reconnoitered near Fort Donelson. Mounted raiders rode alongside trains passing through Sumner County and ambushed Union soldiers who were away from their camps.

CHAPTER 68

The two theatres in Nashville were full every night as citizens, soldiers, and others stood in line to watch the offerings. There was pushing and shoving and the houses were so full—crowds numbered about 1,600—it was hard to breathe but people braved rain, storms, heat and cold because of their hunger for entertainment.

The Howes and Norton Champion Circus, which set up on Market Street near the Louisville and Nashville depot, performed in the afternoons and evenings and attracted huge crowds, which filled the tents early. If you came at starting time or later, you were turned away.

On Thursday, February 11, I took Rachel to see "Othello" at the Nashville Theatre. Starring in the production was John Wilkes Booth in the lead role. Othello must battle Iago, a truly despicable character for the beautiful Desdemona in that tragedy. Iago's lines, "I am not what I am" and "Knavery's plain face is never seen till us'd" and Roderigo's line, "O Damn'd Iago! O inhuman dog" sum up that character pretty well.

Rachel and I both knew the essence of that Shakespearian drama came from Othello being black while Desdemona was white. It was a disturbing thought to imagine a play produced on a Nashville stage like that; it would certainly lead to unimaginable violence so Othello was always performed by a white man. John Wilkes Booth was a handsome actor, who appeared to have not a single drop of black blood in his veins.

During that evening, Rachel gave me news about Mrs. Acklen and her Belmont mansion. Union army officers often came to Belmont during the occupation. It was a beautiful estate, the house was considered a palace and the surrounding land was filled with flowers, magnolia trees and marble statuary. In addition to the flowers and shrubbery in the yard, the estate had two greenhouses filled with plants from all over the world.

Rachel told me she had visited there recently—although she did not tell me why—and was giddy with news that Mrs. Acklen had managed to pull one over on the Feds. It seems that last September Colonel Acklen died at his Angola Plantation in Louisiana; his wife, Adelicia, was in Nashville at the time, staying in their Belmont mansion. Mrs. Acklen went to their Louisiana plantation to check on the estate and, while there, discovered a large quantity of cotton her husband was able to protect from the Confederates, who demanded that he burn it when the Union army approached.

This was a treasure trove the cotton manufacturers in England would love to have, so after the first of the year, Mrs. Acklen employed her charm and savvy to obtain permission from the Confederate States of America to ship the cotton to Liverpool, where it would be sold.

Mrs. Acklen employed Union army teamsters, teams, and wagons to move the cotton to the docks, where river boats loaded and carried it to New Orleans. There, a Yankee broker arranged to ship the 2,000 bales of cotton to Liverpool and Mrs. Acklen received $960,000 in gold for it.

After completing this transaction, Mrs. Acklen took a ship to New York City, then traveled by railroad back to Nashville. She had been gone for eight months, accompanied by her cousin, Mrs. Sarah A. Gaut.

CHAPTER 69

The country was devastated by the loss of young men by the start of 1864. Looking back, it seems obvious there was no way the Confederacy could win this War but it was not ready to surrender, either. The victory at Chickamauga by General Hood, Lee's army's control of the Shenandoah Valley, holding off the seige of Charleston, and the failures of the Union army in the Southwest kept hopes alive for the Confederacy. The fact that the Rebels had held off the Union army, which had better supplies and more men, for three years was a source of hope. Also, Southerners knew that most Northerners wanted the War to end and were open to negotiation, which could lead to independence, and that was another reason for the Southern army to hold on.

Governor Johnson announced in early January that elections for county officials would be held in March; however, before they could vote, each citizen had to take an Oath of Loyalty to the Union that stated they ardently "Desire the suppression of the present insurrection" and favored extension of the Emancipation Proclamation to Tennessee. Known as the "Damnesty Oath" it was more than many loyal Unionists could abide and caused many Tennesseans—even some of Johnson's supporters and friends in East Tennessee—to become embittered with the heavy handed tactics of the Federal government.

By the time the election occurred, over 15,000 had taken the Loyalty Oath but many were women and ineligible to vote.

A significant number lived outside Davidson County. Many took the Oath not because they were loyal but because they wanted to continue to do business in Middle Tennessee so Johnson faced a dilemma: how and where do you find enough loyal men to establish a citizen government in Middle Tennessee?

Once again I took an oath in the hopes that it would somehow protect my sons.

The election turned out to be a farce as the Union slate won the election by a lopsided margin while most eligible voters stayed away from the polls; they knew it was a forgone conclusion before the polls opened.

CHAPTER 70

Governor Johnson showed personal courage when a Union officer shot at him towards the end of May. The officer's name was Lieutenant Augustus Brown and he was with the Seventy-First Ohio Volunteer Infantry. He had just been promoted to First Lieutenant and celebrated by getting profoundly drunk. The young Lieutenant created a disturbance on the street outside Governor Johnson's house—the Governor had been sick and was at home—and when the Governor saw him stagger down the street he confronted him and told him to leave. The officer, who was no doubt too drunk to realize it was the Governor speaking to him, fired his pistol at Johnson and the shot hit the tail of Johnson's coat, then cocked his pistol for a second shot whereupon Johnson rushed at him, threw him on the ground and seized his pistol.

Someone with the Provost Guard heard the shot, came and arrested the soldier, who was charged with serious crimes: firing with intent to kill and conduct unbecoming an officer and a gentleman. The young lieutenant was court-martialed, found guilty and sentenced to be dishonorably discharged. He had to forfeit all his pay and was sentenced to hard labor in prison for three years.

And to think all this came about because he was celebrating a military promotion, no doubt for being a good soldier up to that point!

CHAPTER 71

Governor Johnson was nominated to be Lincoln's vice-president at the Republican Convention in June. When news reached Nashville of Johnson's nomination there were cannons fired from Forts Gillem and Negley and that night cannons were fired from the Capitol grounds. A marching band led a parade from the Capitol to the St. Cloud Hotel, where Johnson spoke to about 2,000 people.

Johnson had been to Washington in December and met with the President. Johnson's embrace of the abolitionist platform angered most local Unionists, who criticized him for accepting the nomination. Even though those Unionists supported Lincoln when it came to seccesion, they were not in accord when it came to freeing slaves and so a number of Unionists went to Chicago and joined the Democratic national nominating convention when it opened in August.

That convention nominated General George McClellan for President. McClellan was the first Commanding General of the Union army and probably had the Democratic nomination in mind when the War started and that's why he didn't press the Rebels too hard. He thought he'd take it easy on them and guarantee his election. The soldiers loved him because he kept them out of battles but you can't win a War that way. Now they had General Grant in charge and I'll bet Grant never thought about being President; he just thought about winning battles and destroying the Confederate army.

General Grant set up his winter headquarters in Nashville. He lived in banker Daniel Carter's home—he stayed in the parlor—which was across the street from his High Street headquarters. General Grant met the Carter family at breakfast one morning and they all described him as very much a gentleman. Of course, Carter's daughter, Rachel Carter Craighead, was the most devoted Rebel sympathizer in the city. She hated the Union army; she was secesh all the way.

When Grant left that house, he paid them for room and board and wrote out an order for the military to protect that home, and they did.

CHAPTER 72

On March 3, 1864 there was an interview with Mrs. Polk in the Nashville Daily Times & True Union. In that interview she "admitted her love of the South but held tightly to the Union—the whole government." She told the reporter she had never been a secessionist and probably could never be one, stating that President Lincoln was constitutionally elected and his election should be recognized by every true patriot. She admitted her "womanly sympathies" were with the South and often caught herself "exulting over the success of Southern arms" but such was the case "only when my reason is taken prisoner and my judgment temporarily suspended at the bidding of my sympathies, prejudices and affections." Her feeling for the South was too deeply ingrained for her to change "And yet, dear sir, notwithstanding all this, I long and pray and yearn for a restoration of my distracted country to its former peaceful and happy condition."

Sarah Polk was as serious about her political work as she was about her religion. President Polk wasn't flashy, wasn't a witty, entertaining conversationalist—but he was certainly hard working. He worked all the time, although his wife made him stop work on Sundays. She made her husband go to church with her, even though he wasn't particularly religious and the religion he did prefer was Methodist. Still, they showed up every Sunday at Mrs. Polk's Presbyterian church fashionably late and made a splashy entrance when they came that no one could miss.

A man needs a supportive wife in order to have a career in politics, someone who works in tandem with his ambition and drive. A political couple is yoked together and they pull as a team to bring that wagon of votes into polling places on election day. Then, during his time in office a politician's wife must be a sounding board for ideas, a fount of caution and wisdom and a source of strength during those dark days that threaten a politician's career and principles.

James Polk had no trusted personal advisers except Sarah. He always called his wife "Mrs. Polk," which indicates that he was a stiff, formal person. But it also indicates his wife was pretty stiff and formal. I'm sure she wanted him to call her that, or else she would have told him to call her something different. Like "Sarah." But he always called her "Mrs. Polk" and so did everyone else. I don't remember anyone calling her anything but "Mrs. Polk" to her face or even behind her back.

CHAPTER 73

In early March, Mrs. Grant joined her husband in Nashville and they moved to a home on McLemore Street. About that same time he went to Washington where President Lincoln named him commanding general of the entire Union army. Before he left, Grant put General Thomas in charge of the army in Nashville.

The first thing Grant did when he returned was issue an order that said his headquarters would be in the field and then left. Now here was a man who would fight and we would soon know how much fight he had in him. General Sherman was a fighter too, and Grant named him his successor as commander of the West.

In early May the Union army under General Sherman began to moved South towards General Joseph Johnston's army; Sherman had about 100,000 men while Johnston had about half that many. Sherman also had a steady stream of supplies coming by rail every day, many from Nashville.

There was something that happened during the War that never failed to intrigue me. There were females disguised as soldiers—Union soldiers are ones I heard about but there were probably Confederate soldiers too—and one female served over two years with the 34th Indiana before she was discovered. It was hard for me to believe that a woman wanted to fight in a War, or that she was even capable of combat and then it amazed me that it took so long to discover a woman was disguised as a soldier.

During a two month period—roughly between mid-January and mid-March, 1864, there were over four thousand refugees sent to Nashville from rural areas where the armies had destroyed farms and homes. Those refugee didn't seem human when they arrived; they had no money and lived in filth and distress, more like animals trying to survive than people and I felt disgust when I saw them. I know I should not feel that way because we are all God's children and I am also aware of "but for the grace of God go I" when it comes to those situations but I could not stop myself.

Those people were poor wretched creatures before the War began who were made even poorer and more wretched because of the War. The women smoked pipes and dipped snuff—you could hardly call them ladies—and they were mostly ignorant and illiterate. Both the men and women seemed incapable of anything other than field work. They were pitiable creatures but they were hard to pity because they were so despised. They were white, but lower than blacks.

In July, General John Bell Hood, who lost his right leg at Chickamauga and the use of his left arm at Gettysburg, replaced General Johnston as commander of the Army of Tennessee. Hood was a tall man—over six feet—who advanced through the ranks from Captain to General because of his success in the field.

Hood was 33 years old but those who knew him criticized him for being "too much of the lion and not enough of the fox" to be in command of an army.

CHAPTER 74

Nashville was known as "the city of harlots" during the Civil War, with almost five hundred registered prostitutes plying their trade. In one of the more memorable events in 1864, a young lady, nude from the waist up, drove up Cherry Street in an open hack. As she passed the Maxwell House, hundreds of soldiers began a lusty cheer that lasted well after she passed.

The wildest and most dangerous place in Nashville was Smokey Row, the area along Second Avenue filled with bars and hookers. Each night that area was so disorderly that half the police force in Nashville was required to keep some semblance of order. There were fights and shootings and every night saw citizens, soldiers and women arrested.

CHAPTER 75

At the end of August, General Wheeler's cavalry—about 4,000 strong—rode into Middle Tennessee and rumors quickly spread that he was headed for Nashville. Actually, there were a number of rumors about Wheeler: that he had been captured at Murfreesboro, that he had captured Union prisoners, that he was leading an invasion of Kentucky and that he had 12,000 men with him. The rumors were so prevalent that a number of women and children in Gallatin and Sumner County moved into Nashville to escape the expected carnage.

In early September, General Rousseau left Nashville in pursuit of General Wheeler and found him about 20 miles south of Nashville in LaVergne. There was some skirmishing—citizens in Nashville heard the gunfire—and Wheeler's troops drove the Union forces back toward the city and inflicted heavy casualties.

Wheeler continued to harass the Union army, inflicting heavy damage on rail lines connecting Nashville with Chattanooga. Wheeler's men cut telegraph lines, burned railroad cross ties and heated rails so they could bend them into "neckties," which were rails wrapped around posts. This put pressure on Sherman to protect his supply lines and slowed his movement towards Atlanta while giving relief to Hood. Union forces were unaware that Wheeler only had a force of 2,500.

CHAPTER 76

In September, the Army of Tennessee was about 20 miles southwest of the Georgia line and the soldiers were pretty fed up with General Hood. They needed basics like shoes, clothing, weapons, ammunition and food to keep fighting but none were coming. Some of the men hadn't been paid for a year and a number of soldiers slipped away for home. It was not a good time for the Confederate army, which was burdened with a General they deemed to be incompetent.

General Sherman led his army towards Hood and in late September, Hood maneuvered his army around Sherman's right and struck the railroad south of Chattanooga. Sherman followed Hood's army wherever it went, but Hood was an enigma whose erratic leadership caused Sherman to wonder what he was up to. Hood's troops wondered the same thing. Sherman reportedly said that Hood was nothing like General Johnston "who was a sensible man and only did sensible things."

Nashville was key to Sherman's operation because the General depended on supplies coming from Nashville to support his army. The fact that they did it so well was in large part responsible for the success of Sherman's army, which captured Atlanta and burned it in early September.

Back in Nashville, news arrived about the fall of Atlanta, which caused celebrations by Unionists with cannons firing. A number of refugees fleeing Atlanta headed toward Nashville.

Meanwhile, General Rousseau continued to follow Wheeler's troops and skirmish. There were fights south of Franklin and then Rousseau followed Wheeler to Athens, Alabama but could not catch him. Wheeler decided to join General Hood in Georgia and set off in that direction.

On Sunday, September 11, a day of prayer and thanksgiving was declared because of recent victories by the Union army at Atlanta and the Union navy at Mobile Bay. Union supporters cheered but Rebel sympathizers wept at news that Confederate Cavalry leader General John Hunt Morgan was killed in Greenville, near Knoxville. When I heard the news I immediately thought of Robert and wondered about his safety.

The next evening, there was a one hundred gun salute at night and government buildings were festooned with red, white and blue bunting. That evening, church bells were rung by Unionists and Governor Johnson delivered a victory speech.

The euphoria of patriotism turned to anger when Governor Johnson ordered all males between the ages of 18 and 50—black and white—to register for military duty. His proposal to form a military force to protect the city against guerillas was met with hostility and men refused to enroll. One of those who did enroll was 62-year old William Driver.

CHAPTER 77

Most people thought Abe Lincoln was a failure; the War was dragging on and nobody was winning and a lot of good, young men had died. General John C. Freemont declared his candidacy, but in September he withdrew. The election of 1864 looked to be quite interesting.

The Unionists never failed to punish with their distortions. On September 23, a rally was held at Fort Gillem for the Lincoln-Johnson ticket and to adopt a resolution for the abolition of slavery. The vote was 870 to 5 in favor of this. Three days later the Constitutional Union Club met and voted their support to General McClellan but on the twenty-seventh there was a torchlight parade for the Lincoln-Johnson ticket and Governor Johnson addressed the crowd.

Governor Johnson knew better than to hold elections for local offices in Nashville because Confederate supporters would win hands down. So for the third straight year he appointed the councilmen and alderman for the city. That not only helped him keep control of the city, it also helped in his campaign for the Lincoln-Johnson ticket.

At the end of September, Johnson issued a proclamation calling for the first Tuesday after the first Monday in November—the eighth—to be the date for the Presidential election. White males over 21 years of age who had lived in Tennessee for at least six months before the election and had taken the Loyalty Oath were qualified to vote. Johnson issued his proclamation to free Negroes but he didn't want them to vote. He also didn't want them to get the idea they were social equals with white citizens.

Johnson was not subtle. His proclamation made it an act of treason to vote for McClellan.

At the end of September, I had dinner with Rachel, who was filled with news about young ladies marrying Yankees. That month Mary Florence Kirkham married a Union captain and Miss Kirkham's mother was appalled. "She thinks that of all the hardships she's had to endure, this is the worst," said Rachel. She told me that Laura Ewing and Berta McGavock had both married Yankee soldiers too but most of the young women were aghast at the thought.

"But aren't you seeing a young Union Lieutenant?" I asked Rachel. She smiled and said "but that's different." She acknowledged he was kind, considerate and handsome—"a gentleman"—but that was to gain information to help the Confederate army. I had seen her with this young Lieutenant a time or two and she always smiled and looked flirtatious. I knew she gained information from him but wondered how her affections could remain neutral.

A young woman needs a young man as a companion. I believed Rachel, but thought that she might be deceiving herself by thinking her heart could not be captured by a handsome young man, no matter what uniform he wore. Still, I hoped that she and Edward might find their way together after the War.

CHAPTER 78

By the end of September, General Forrest had crossed the Tennessee River and vowed to remain in the area until General Sherman came out of Atlanta for a fight. Forrest had a force of about 8,000 and my spies told me the Union army thought he was headed to Nashville so they sent about 2,000 soldiers to keep an eye on him. General Forrest's moves excited the members of the Nashville community.

Forrest came north toward Pulaski, about 80 miles south of Nashville, where General Rousseau waited. The Union army fell back toward Nashville as Forrest headed towards Fayetteville, about 50 miles south of Nashville. This move caused the Union army to retreat towards Nashville.

General Sherman would have nothing to do with these maneuvers. He stayed in Atlanta.

Meanwhile, Forrest did extensive damage to the Tennessee and Alabama Railroad between Pulaski and Athens, Alabama. He and his troops burned all the bridges and trestle works before moving east toward the Nashville and Chattanooga Railroad, which was Sherman's main artery for supplies.

The State Capitol—"Fort Andrew Johnson"—was surrounded by field guns and earthworks while the lower floors had stockades around them. Up on Casino Hill there was a blockhouse while Fort Gillem, located in North Nashville, held the powder magazine for the city.

Down in Chattanooga, General Thomas sent General Rousseau, who was in Tullahoma, to Nashville to help defend against Forrest. Rousseau arrived in Nashville on October 2 and issued an order for every horse and mule in the city. The Union army commandeered horses and mules from stables and citizens.

There were telegrams saying that Forrest was in Huntsville, Alabama as well as Spring Hill and Fayetteville, Tennessee. Somebody was wrong.

Meanwhile, the citizens of Atlanta who saw their city burned by Sherman were coming in droves daily to Nashville. There were also a number of Confederate prisoners sent to Nashville before being shipped to prison camps, mostly in the midwest. There were always Rebel prisoners in Nashville and their marching through the city was a depressing sight.

General Forrest became aware of the Federal army's maneuvers to capture his cavalry and, afraid of being trapped by the rising Tennessee River, abandoned his plans for Middle Tennessee. In early October, Forrest headed south towards the Tennessee River.

The Union army was worried about him. A telegram reported he had captured Columbia, cut telegraph lines along the Nashville and Chattanooga Railroad line south of Murfreesboro and seemed to roam through the countryside at will. The truth was that Forrest had not taken Columbia but had captured three blockhouses between Franklin and Columbia on the Tennessee and Alabama Railroad line.

Generals Rousseau and Thomas set out to trap Forrest, who had to cross the Tennessee River at Pride's Ferry. Union commanders said the river was too high to be forded. Another report had Forrest over the Alabama line, but in reality, nobody in Nashville knew where he was or where he was headed. Many believed he was headed towards Middle Tennessee on his way to Kentucky and both citizens and soldiers prepared for a battle in Nashville.

In mid-October, General Rousseau led his troops back into Nashville after failing to find Forrest. The citizens of Nashville had been excited in anticipation of Confederate forces entering the city but were disappointed that Forrest had not continued his drive into Nashville. Instead, more fresh Union troops arrived.

CHAPTER 79

The weather was horrible; rain, rain and more rain which made mud, mud and more mud. For the soldiers who had to march, march and march some more, it was a back-breaking ordeal, especially since food was scarce. Those soldiers would go 24 hours without food, marching on a meal short on meat. Even worst for some soldiers was that they were running short on tobacco.

Rachel came by with a letter from Edward, which had been passed to her from her friends, that told me of those conditions. He noted he was well but Rebel soldiers were short on shoes, coats, blankets, food and just about everything. Although Edward said he was doing fine, I wondered how much he was suffering. I resolved to find a blanket and warm clothes for him.

After giving me the letter from Edward, Rachel told me the Rebel army was in Gadsden, Alabama, where General Hood informed General Beauregard he planned to move toward Nashville with hopes of ending up in Kentucky. Beauregard had doubts about Hood's plans; he thought they were formulated carelessly. General Beauregard finally gave his approval of the operation but, according to Rachel, thought Hood's operation was rushed and based on luck.

On October 21, G.W. Ashburn of Georgia spoke for about an hour at the Nashville Courthouse before a rally for McClellan. The rally was broken up by soldiers armed with sabers, carbines and pistols who ran in, doused the lights and ordered the crowd to disperse.

As the crowd ran for the exits, they heard shouts of "Johnson and Lincoln!" Soldiers from East Tennessee took credit for breaking up the event.

On the evening of October 24, Negroes carried torches in a parade to the Capitol where Governor Johnson promised "freedom, full, broad and unconditional, to every man in Tennessee."

It was a red meat speech with Johnson singling out William Harding and Mark Cockrill, owners of two of the largest plantations in Middle Tennessee, and stating their land should be divied up "and parcelled out amongst a number of free, industrious, and honest farmers."

Johnson said he wanted an end to black "concubinage..to satisfy the brutal lusts of slaveholders and overseers" and to see that the "sanctity of God's holy law of marriage shall be respected in your persons." When he said he hoped a Moses might arise to lead them to their promised land of freedom and happiness, several members of the Negro crowd shouted "You are our Moses." Johnson demurred, briefly, then announced, "If no better shall be found, I will indeed be your Moses and lead you through the Red Sea of War and bondage to a fairer future of liberty and peace."

The slaves in Tennessee freed themselves because the War took a toll on the way of life that kept them slaves. The old aristocracy lost its power and, as slaves realized this, they proclaimed themselves free. Negroes resisted their owners because the owners really couldn't enforce their power. Slaves could talk back to their owners, refuse orders and avoid punishment and retaliation. Freedom is a state of mind and increasingly the Negroes held the belief they were free. They declared they were free because slave owners could not declare they were not and enforce it. Some of the slave owners had gone South, or joined the Confederate army, or stayed home and tried to hold on to their land. They could bark but they couldn't bite and when you can't bite, you have to stop barking. It was a come-down for those former masters, a huge dose of humiliation that was hard for them to swallow.

CHAPTER 80

All during 1864 the War was part of everyday life. There were military personnel moving in and out of the city in large numbers, prisoners of War marching into the city to be held until they were shipped to prison camps, and citizens—black and white—coming into the city. The city itself changed; there were more fortifications and defense lines established and supply depots held more goods.

The realization that the South was losing the War came slowly, in fits and starts, but it came to more and more as time passed and opportunities were lost to rid the South of the hated Yankee army. Nashville citizens were frustrated and disappointed on one hand, but relieved on the other because the large Federal presence kept the city from being destroyed. Some even dared to think ahead and saw a future where Nashville might become "normal" again, with city and county elections and a society where citizens lived without constant conflict with the Union army, which took mules and horses and disrupted daily life.

Maybe that's the reason that, throughout the year, more Nashvillians signed the Oath of Allegiance. Many were reluctant to sign earlier, as they continued to hold onto hope that the Confederacy would prevail, but by the Fall of 1864, there was little hope left. The bursts of optimism and hope that did occur seemed more like fireworks shot into the sky, which glowed brightly for a moment, then disappeared.

The citizens of Nashville had been on edge for three years, hearing over and over that the Confederate army was headed this way, that Confederate victories were imminent, that General Forrest would arrive at any time and, with one of his miracles, free the city. All those rumors had proven to be false and when someone has lived in anticipation for three years and had their hopes dashed time and again, it's hard to get hopes up again. There was still a glimmer of hope, but it was a small burning ember, not a huge flame licking the sky.

Down in Georgia, General Sherman left Atlanta in the middle of November and headed East, burning a path 60 miles wide from there to Savannah. That march to the sea destroyed everything in its way. General Sherman may have thought he was just lighting fires on Georgia's land, but in fact he was lighting a fire inside each citizen of Georgia that would burn with hatred against him for the rest of their lives and their children's lives and on down for generations. After that beastly act, if your name happened to be Sherman and you lived in Georgia, you'd better change your name.

General Sherman didn't just ruin a part of Georgia, he ruined any hopes of forgiveness from those in Georgia who saw or felt or even knew what he had done. There is a vicious meanness to fire that tortures before it eats everything in its path. Georgia was a torture chamber and Sherman and his Union army were the executioners who killed the spirit of the people of that great state.

Nashville witnessed the fruits of Sherman's actions when prisoners of War captured by the Union army arrived in the city for transfer to northern prisons. Almost every day, prisoners arrived, as well as a ragtag mass of people who had lost everything and needed protection against the elements and an army that destroyed homes, barns, fences, crops and animals.

CHAPTER 81

The Presidential election was held on November 8, 1864 and three days before that date there was a large torchlight parade that marched for the Lincoln-Johnson ticket. The streets of downtown Nashville were filled with people—mostly Union soldiers or government employees—who saw fireworks at the Capitol and heard guns being fired. It was a big crowd, but there were few native Nashville citizens in it.

There was a victory celebration planned for the evening of the election but heavy rains hit the city so there was no parade. Two days after the election, the results showed Lincoln a clear victor over McClellan, who only collected 25 votes. Civilian employees of the government who had been in Nashville for six months constituted the bulk of voters. On the evening of November 12, there was a victory celebration with a torchlight parade, a number of military bands, fireworks and guns fired in praise of the Lincoln-Johnson ticket.

On October 30, some of General Hood's troops had crossed the Tennessee River at Florence, Alabama and moved North towards Nashville. In the advance guard was former Tennessee Governor Isham Harris.

In early November, General Forrest destroyed the Union river depot at Johnsonville and three Union gunboats as well as transports carrying government freight. Forrest would have captured goods stored there but Union soldiers burned their own transports and warehouses to stop them from being captured by Rebels. Nashvillians learned of this when people fleeing that area came into the city.

The Daily Press reported that General Hood led his army out of Gadsden, Alabama and was headed towards Nashville. A week later, Hood's army crossed the Tennessee River. Hood and his army spent three weeks in Northern Alabama, repairing the railroad tracks from Corinth, searching for supplies and waiting for General Forrest and his cavalry to return from their Johnsonville raid.

CHAPTER 82

Rachel had a concerned look on her face when I came down to the dining room at the St. Cloud one evening. She was dining with her mother and beckoned me over and told me she had a very unusual experience that day. She said she saw Matthew from time to time on the street and they always acknowledged each other but never talked. On this day, Matthew came over to her and whispered "Tell Robert to be careful" then quickly walked away.

Rachel told me some of her friends had seen Edward when they visited Forrest's camp and he was well. She said her friends told her General Hood planned to capture Nashville, seize the Federal supplies stored here, attract Tennessee volunteers to his ranks, then drive north through Kentucky and into Ohio. However, there was a delay in Northern Alabama which allowed General Thomas to prepare Nashville defenses against an attack. Rachel said other Rebel Generals—she did not name them—thought Hood's plan "was more a flight of fantasy, totally devoid of reality but, at that point, the only vision of glory available to the General and his troops."

If a military campaign based on fantasy weren't bad enough, the Confederate army had to face a day of snow and sleet followed by a day of rain which meant they marched over frozen ice one day and through mud the next. On Tuesday, November 22 a cold, sharp wind drove snow into the faces of Rebel soldiers marching over frozen ground. The troops marched about 18 miles that day, finally crossing the state line into Tennessee.

On the morning of November 24, General Cox led his Union troops to a crossroads a couple miles south of Columbia where they stopped Forrest's cavalry. Around ten that morning, General Schofield led Union troops into Columbia and dug earthworks facing South.

Back in Nashville, it was quiet and calm because President Lincoln had issued a proclamation for a national day of thanksgiving and prayer. This first Thanksgiving was held in army installations, government offices, shops and warehouses—but there were no festivities.

There was plenty of activity the next night in Smokey Row. Soldiers from a Union infantry unit went there looking to satisfy their carnal urges when they ran into units comprised of volunteers. The men got in an argument about which was better—regulars or volunteers—and somewhere along the way forgot about satisfying their carnal desires and began fighting. It was a massive brawl, with fists as well as bullets flying. The police arrived and arrested about twenty.

A sense of pessimism permeated Southerners to the point where they openly wondered if we could win this War or not. At the Battle of Stones River in Murfreesboro, many believed the Southern army lost a great opportunity and the army's high command was blamed. Edward told me that General Braxton Bragg was not held in high esteem by many serving under his command. At the Battle of Chickamauga, he was blamed for that loss and some of his Generals actively sought to have him removed from command.

Those under his command grew to hate him and hold him in contempt and did not hide their feelings, according to Edward. The General-in-Chief did not have the confidence of his Generals. President Davis was in a pinch. He had a long friendship with both General Bragg and General Polk but those two Generals could not get along. Polk swore he'd never again serve under Bragg and Bragg made it clear he didn't want Polk in his army.

After the Southern army was defeated at the Battle of Chattanooga, General Bragg was relieved from his command and replaced by General Joe Johnston, who was popular with the troops. General Hood would not accept any blame for his failures. The truth, said Edward, was that Hood was a lousy administrator and poor at dealing with logistics.

CHAPTER 83

A few nights later—it was after midnight—I was awakened by sharp knocks on my door, then footsteps that walked quickly away. I got out of bed and found a note slid under the door. Lighting a candle, I read "Urgent. Go to the shed on Cherry Street by the railroad depot." I vaguely remembered seeing a shed down there.

I wondered if I should go; if the police found someone prowling around the train depot at that time of night they'd no doubt arrest him, and I had been very careful to never allow myself to be exposed like this. But I thought about Robert and Edward, that they might need me, so I dressed quickly and left the hotel.

I walked cautiously down Commerce Street, weaved my way around as I headed towards the train station. After about 20 minutes of walking, I saw the shed and approached cautiously. The door was slightly ajar and I pushed it in a bit further. There was a body hanging there, his hands tied behind his back, the rope around his neck fastened to a wooden beam. It was Robert.

My breath was trapped in my throat and I let out a small "ughh." I went over and put my arms around Robert and broke into uncontrolled sobs. He was not stiff, which meant he had not been dead for long. I lifted him up, hoping to ease the strain on his neck, and then put him down. I looked up and wondered how I would get him down; I needed a knife but did not have one. I knew I needed something to stand on but I just stood there, hugging Robert and sobbing.

I did not hear Matthew come in the door, but he put his hand on my back, pulled up a keg, mounted and, with a quick swipe of his knife at the rope, cut him down. Matthew helped me hold the body and said "let's go outside." I was surprised that Matthew was there, and thankful but my mind was a blur. I had gone from deep sobs to a numbness; I did not ask Matthew why he was there or how he knew about Robert.

A policeman stuck his head in the door, gun drawn, holding a lantern, and said "what's going on?" I said "My son is dead." That's all I said; that's all I could think to say. Matthew said, "It's O.K. We're going put him in a wagon." A wagon drawn by a horse was brought up and Matthew and I laid Robert on that wagon. I did not question any of this; I was paralyzed with grief. "We'll take him to the undertaker," said Matthew and all I could do was nod in agreement.

It took about an hour to get to the undertaker and I spent that entire time with my head buried on Robert; I could not stop sobbing, muttering "oh no, oh no." At the undertaker, the body was carried inside and put on a table. I told the man, "I need to bury my son" and he just nodded. I do not remember Matthew or the horse drawn wagon leaving. I was sitting with my head in my hands when I realized the eastern sky was beginning to show a sliver of light and I stood up. By that time the undertaker had placed Robert in a coffin.

"We'll have to bury him quickly," he said, and I nodded. "I'll need to notify the church about a funeral," I said but the undertaker said "we don't have time for that. We have to bury him this morning."

"But why?" I asked. "Can't he have a proper burial? A church burial?"

"Mr. Duncan," he said, "the Union army would not allow that." I well knew that Robert had been working for the Rebels but I kept believing, deep down, that the Feds did not know it. That Robert was careful and took no great risks. That Robert was, well—I had no great logic to my thoughts. Robert was my son and that's all the logic I had.

It had been light for less than an hour when Robert was laid in a grave in the City Cemetery. I don't know how Rachel found out but she was there with me; she arrived after the coffin had arrived at the cemetery. She and I and the undertaker, along with a gravedigger, were the only ones who witnessed the burial of Robert Duncan. His grave was not marked. I wondered why Matthew was not there, too, but the hurt was so deep that I could not think clearly or find an explanation.

There is no grief as deep as the grief of a man who has lost his son. I expected Robert to be around when I was in my old age, although I never thought about it like that. I assumed I would die before Robert did, but I never really gave that much thought, either. There was a weariness, a heaviness that I carried as I walked from the grave. I felt nothing and yet I would begin a deep sobbing I could not stop, then that would leave and I remembered times from his childhood, him playing with his brothers, throwing rocks at a tree, fishing, his smile, lying in bed asleep when I came home late, just being alive and part of my life. I could not fathom how I would ever endure this, if I would ever get over Robert's death—I did not want to ever get over Robert's death—and how I would ever face another day.

I thought about Edward and Matthew and wondered about them; mostly I wondered about Edward, out with General Forrest, riding around the countryside, taunting Fed soldiers, luring them into a fight.

I went back to my room at the St. Cloud and stayed in bed all that day. I did not get up until noon the next day. I was not hungry but I went to the dining room and ate a meal. The numbness had receded and I knew I would face the day. By the middle of that afternoon, I was engaged in conversations with others.

I remember walking back to the hotel with Rachel, who cautioned me to not mention this to anyone. Other than that, I do not remember if we talked or what we said. I do not remember her leaving me. When I saw her again, at dinner, I asked "Does Edward know?" She shook her head and said, quietly, "No."

"Will you get the message to him?" I asked.

She just looked at me and did not answer. I walked away.

CHAPTER 84

Citizens of Nashville who supported the Southern cause were once again optimistic in late November when it was reported that General Hood was at or near Columbia, about 45 miles south of town. Reports were that General Hood had promised his men they'd soon see Louisville.

On the morning of November 30, Rachel, Mrs. Monahan and I had breakfast at the St. Cloud and Rachel was furious. She had received news from her friends that three days previous, General Hood set up his headquarters at "Beechlawn," the plantation owned by Amos and Cornelia Warfield, located about three miles south of Columbia. General Hood planned to cross the Duck River and strike north. He ordered General Forrest to lead his cavalry across the river so a bridge could be constructed to allow infantry to cross.

General Forrest crossed the river, maneuvered around Union cavalry and headed toward Spring Hill. By 9:30 the next morning, about 20,000 Confederate troops had crossed the Duck River and were marching north but they discovered it was almost 20 miles to Spring Hill instead of 12, which the map showed.

The Union army was dug in at Spring Hill and General Hood was in a foul mood; he had fallen off his horse, which made his old wounds flare up and caused him great pain. He didn't know where the Union army was positioned or how many there were but he owned a big advantage: General Hood's army was between the Union army and the road to Nashville.

"Hood's army could have crushed the Feds," said Rachel. "But the Rebs decided to enjoy a relaxing evening."

Nobody doubted General Frank Cheatham's dedication and devotion to the Southern cause, or that his men seemed to like him, but he came up short as a commander. He swore much and often and drank the same way. There were stories he was so drunk at the Battle of Stone's River that he fell off his horse when he tried to lead his men into battle. He was a fierce fighter, drunk or sober, although commanding a corps seemed to be beyond his level of competence.

According to Rachel, General Cheatham was fully drunk that evening, which was spent by Confederate officers in Rippaville, the home belonging to Nathaniel Cheairs where the William McKissacks lived. The officers were eating, drinking and offering toasts to each other, to the Southern cause, and to their comrades in arms. Pretty Jessie Peters was there, "the same Jessie Peters whose attraction to Earl Van Dorn had cost him his life," said Rachel, "but Mrs. Peters' husband was not. There may have been a romantic escapade between Mrs. Peters and General Cheatham, and maybe between her and more than one Confederate officer. At least that's what some have told me. And General Hood may have drunk past the point of sobriety."

General Hood spent that night at the home of Absalom Thompson in Spring Hill, where he received a note from Governor Isham Harris around six that evening to block the Columbia-Franklin Pike. During the evening, Generals Cheatham, Forrest, Cleburne and

Bate all visited with Hood but no one occupied that road to Nashville or, apparently, was ordered to occupy that road. Hood reportedly asked Stewart about the Pike but Stewart replied he didn't control the road. Hood asked him to send troops to block the road but Stewart said his troops were tired and hungry and were going to set up camp and get some rest.

During that night "the Union army marched up that road toward Franklin and Nashville while those Generals and the entire Rebel army slept," fumed Rachel. "Those Feds could see the Rebel campfires as they marched past. But the Rebel army never woke up or fired a shot into that line of Feds marching past."

Rachel was so incensed she could hardly eat her food as she spoke in whispers.

"When the Rebel army woke up, the Union army was in Franklin," she said. "General Hood was furious and berated his Generals for letting that happen. His temper was on high boil and the Generals he accused of letting this happen defended themselves and demanded apologies!"

"If there was a book about how to not run an army, Hood could've written it," said Rachel. "He should have stayed up and made sure something like that did not happen. And General Cheatham," she said as she shook with anger. "I'm fully aware that the charms of a Mrs. Peters are difficult to refuse when she sets her sight on a healthy man and General Cheatham was not known as a man who was even remotely willing to resist the charms of any woman, much less one as charming and determined as Mrs. Peters."

That morning was bright and warm, an Indian summer day that would have been perfect for a picnic. The temperature rose as the day rolled on. I wondered what would happen if General Hood's army moved toward Nashville, which I presumed was his intention.

As Rachel and I walked that morning we found that General Thomas had stopped all trains travelling on the Nashville and Chattanooga as well as the Nashville and Northwestern railroad lines and ordered all passengers on the Louisville and Nashville Road coming into Nashville be denied accomodations. At the Nashville wharf we saw a large number of Navy ships and throughout the city men were digging trenches and building earthen fortifications.

CHAPTER 85

Through the years I spoke with a number of soldiers and others who had been at Franklin during that battle and they are my sources for this account.

It was just before noon on November 30 when General Hood rode up to the home of William Harrison, dismounted and hobbled through the front door with his crutch and rested for a spell. Hood was still fuming at the previous night's events and directed his anger at both his troops and his officers. His men needed a lesson, a rebuke for what they had allowed to happen, a jolt to wake them to their duty as men and soldiers. The men needed discipline. He would give them a lesson in how an army should fight. General Hood knew that General Johnston had the men build breastworks, but he felt breastworks made men too timid and cautious. A real soldier charged the enemy and his army, by God, would charge the Union army in a frontal assault and break that Federal line and then march on to Nashville and take that city.

Around four that afternoon, Confederate officers yelled "Forward" and in picture perfect style about 18,000 Confederate troops, boosted by an eleven man band playing "The Bonnie Blue Flag," carrying torn and tattered battle flags behind officers with gleaming swords leading them on horseback, moved forward. This charge had more men than the Gettysburg charge by General Pickett.

In Nashville, we heard sounds of the battle. The sound of those cannons was like a big bass drum and we thought that sound was the sound of the Rebel army marching into our city. This is what the citizens had expected for three years—the Confederates right outside our city, ready to move in, whip the Federals and give us back our city and our way of life. Oh, it was a sweet, sweet sound to so many in Nashville.

At nine that night, a telegram arrived at the St. Cloud for General George Thomas, informing him the Union army had defeated the Confederates at Franklin.

The fighting in Franklin had continued until after nine and General Hood believed he won the battle. He thought he'd lead the Rebel army into Nashville the next day and told the artillery to open fire on the Federal army first thing the next morning. He didn't know the Union army had pulled out and was marching to Nashville.

It was a bloody, bloody battlefield in Franklin. Six Generals were killed there: Cleburne, Gist, Granbury, Adams, Strahl and Carter. Five other Generals were wounded bad enough to never fight again and one General was captured by the Yanks.

The saddest story of all was Captain Tad Carter, who fought outside the home of his family. Union General Cox made the Carter House his headquarters and the Carter Family—Tad's parents and sisters—were in the basement during that battle. Young Carter hadn't seen his home in over two years. He was shot just a short distance from the house and his father and some other family members found him, brought him inside and laid him in his own bed where he died. If you thought War didn't have cruel twists and turns, you didn't know about Captain Tod Carter.

At Carnton, the plantation owned by the McGavocks, a hospital was set up and Carrie McGavock was an angel, taking care of the sick and wounded. There were four Confederate Generals laid out on her porch—Patrick Cleburne, John Adams, Hiram Granbury and Otto Strahl.

CHAPTER 86

Before the War ended, there were a number of citizens in Nashville who attended church, balls and held teas with Yankee soldiers. Nashville was a rowdy town, full of every kind of human you can name—thieves, drunks, prostitutes, con men and murderers—and many of the good citizens had declared more than once that it was rotten as rotten could be, both morally and socially. It was disorderly and violent and filled with the dregs of humanity. It was a city that had given up its morals, ethics and decency and become a degenerate whore itself. You saw a society that had been devastated, that had been ruined and ravaged by War, even though the armies had not fought a battle here.

As the Union army marched north toward Nashville after the Battle of Franklin they passed the home of Nicholas Edwin Perkins, known as "Meeting of the Waters," which was on the Del Rio Pike headed into Nashville. It was an impressive house, large white pillars on the front, built like the great home on a plantation should be built, right where the West Harpeth and Big Harpeth Rivers come together, and it caught the eye of Union soldiers as they marched from Franklin to Nashville. Those soldiers decided to raid and plunder that house, steal whatever they could and then burn it down, but Perkins made up his mind to save his home.

Perkins' right hand was crippled from a duel with another student when they both attended Centre College in Danville, Kentucky. But hand or no hand, Perkins was determined to defend his property. He locked his wife and daughter in an upstairs room and sent his son to find a Union officer to help him fend off this rogue band of terrorists. The son found a Union officer who came to the house, drew his sword and ran those misfits off. Perkins offered his left hand to shake the officer's hand as a debt of gratitude and realized at that moment that the officer who saved his home was the very same man who crippled his hand years before back in college. Such were the fates of those in this War.

CHAPTER 87

In the 25 years since that War, there have been histories written about the Battle of Nashville and I have drawn on these to construct this history. I lived in Nashville during this time, and talked with a number of people who moved about the city. Since that battle, I have talked with men who were involved in the planning and fighting of that battle, from common soldiers on both sides to officers and this history is a compendium of many sources of information. I hope that I do it justice.

The morning of December 1 was bright and sunny with a sharp chill in the air. On both sides of the Columbia-Franklin Pike in Franklin, men lay everywhere, some dead, some wounded but none who would fight again in this War. There were bodies stacked on bodies in trenches until the pile almost reached the top of the breastworks. There were dead horses laying all over the field and as the sun rose soldiers and volunteers dug graves. Sometimes they dug a long trench and laid bodies side by side, sometimes piled on top of each other. It wasn't right to bury a Union solider and Confederate soldier in the same grave but sometimes it happened. Men took wooden boards and marked some of the graves, scratched out information as best they could about who was buried there but many of those graves were never marked and after awhile nobody even knew somebody was buried there.

In Nashville, the Feds were confident about their defensive positions and optimistic they would defeat the Rebel army. There were over 50,000 Union soldiers in Nashville ready to defend the city. The major fear of the Union command was that General Forrest would come into the city from the north while their attention was directed south toward General Hood, coming up from Franklin.

There are eight roads leading into Nashville—the Nolensville, Franklin, Granny White and Hillsboro Pikes brought the Rebel army in from the South, but there were no Rebels coming down the Lebanon and Murfreesboro Pikes from the east or Charlotte and Harding Pikes from the West.

General Hood sat in the saddle with his one leg and one arm, carrying the attitude that his army had won the Battle of Franklin. That's what he conveyed to the government in Richmond when he telegraphed his report about the Franklin battle, but he neglected to inform Richmond of his considerable losses. Like his army, General Hood was wounded and hurting. There were, at most, 25,000 men under his command, which meant the Union army in Nashville had a two to one advantage over him.

By noon, the Union outer defense line was positioned around Nashville. General Hood positioned his troops just beyond the range of Union artillery and went to Travellers' Rest, the home of John Overton, where he established his command headquarters. A group of young ladies welcomed his arrival and prepared a meal.

Hood lost veteran commanders in Franklin and had to depend on relatively inexperienced men to command troops in Nashville. The Rebels dug breastworks and established a line of defense. At the St. Cloud I overheard Federal officers wondering about his plan of action. Several ideas were debated; some thought Hood intended to skirt Nashville and head towards Kentucky or East Tennessee, cut off the Louisville and Nashville railroad and lay siege to the city; others thought he planned to wait for Union forces to attack him.

Hood sent Generals Forrest and Bates to Murfreesboro to destroy the railroad line into Nashville and burn all bridges.

As the day grew longer, it grew colder.

CHAPTER 88

By the third of December the battle lines were set. There were two lines of defense set up by the Union army with the outside line positioned in an arc from the Cumberland River on the East of the city to that same river on the west of the city. The inner circle was anchored by the Forts; from Fort Negley on St. Cloud Hill to Fort Gillem in North Nashville. The Rebels didn't have as many troops so their line was shorter; it extended from Murfreesboro Pike over to Hillsboro Pike.

General Thomas ordered all men—white or Negro—found unemployed or loafing to work on fortifications around the city. On the hill where the Capitol sat, citizens gathered to view the two armies positioned opposite each other.

On December third and fourth, the armies watched each other while the citizens of Nashville watched, waiting for something to happen. The Union soldiers waited for the Rebels to attack; they thought a charge would happen at any minute but the Rebels stayed in place. It seemed like each army was taking the measure of the other, like two fighters circling before they threw their punches.

On the fourth there were a number of citizens on Capitol Hill who could see the Confederate army. The New York Times reported the Confederates had over 50,000 troops but, truth was, there was less than half that number and those poor men were starving. Still,

General Thomas added thousands more men into the lines of the Federal defenses.

The Union artillery sent shells towards the Rebs but the Rebels didn't fire back. On Sunday, the fifth, you could hear the Federal's cannons loud and clear. They blasted Dr. Buckley's house on Granny White Pike and Joseph Vaulk's house on Franklin Pike and sent shells into the woods and onto the tops of hills, trying to destroy whatever cover the Confederate army had. Both armies raided houses and the Union army swept through Nashville taking horses, saddles and blankets. A travelling circus that was in town lost their trick riding horses and Governor Johnson's bay horses that pulled his carriage were taken as well. The Governor did not care for that one bit.

On the Confederate side, General Isham Harris told the troops they'd be inside Nashville in ten days and at that time could visit their friends and get revenge on their enemies. Nashville was crawling with Union soldiers. The citizens who wandered towards the lines found themselves handed a pick and shovel and ordered to dig entrenchments. Many were Confederate sympathizers who did not care to be digging breastworks for the Union army. Those citizens worked until dark, digging. Meanwhile, fences were torn down, homes and barns were raided and soldiers camped in the yards of residents.

On Monday, the sixth, there was some gunfire and a little fighting during the day but the Confederates spent most of their time digging earthworks and trenches for defense. The Union army continued to believe that Hood would attack and, when he did, the Union line would be in a strong defensive position. However, as time rolled on, the Feds were less sure of an attack and wondered if Hood was going to skirt around Nashville and head toward Kentucky. The editor of the Daily Press wrote that Hood "was too weak to attack and too tired to run away."

On Tuesday the seventh nothing changed; the armies still sat staring at each other. Each side did reconnaissance and Nashville citizens could see Rebel campfires just outside Union lines. It was pretty easy for Rebel soldiers to slip in and out of town and many did so but seventeen Rebel soldiers who came into the city were captured.

The next day, the eighth, Forrest's troops tore up rails so trains could not bring supplies to the Union army. Although Forrest wreaked havoc on the Union army, terrorizing them, the Murfreesboro garrison managed to keep Forrest and his cavalry occuppied so he could not get to Nashville. There were a lot of people who thought Forrest should be in Nashville—was needed in Nashville—but Forrest never arrived.

The weather had been mild but on the eighth it turned a hard, biting cold and rain turned into sleet and snow. The temperature dropped to around ten degrees and the ground froze and was covered with ice. Nobody could move; men and horses in both armies slipped and slid and fell. The whole countryside was paralyzed.

The river had fallen quite a bit in a short amount of time so boats were unable to navigate between Clarksville and Nashville. The Confederates burned bridges and blocked the tunnel north of Nashville so the Union army was now isolated. Federal cannons kept firing and the home of F.R. Rains, situated between the two armies, was demolished and he was killed. Rains had killed a Union soldier earlier that day, so Federal artillery turned their cannons on him and his house in an act of revenge.

The Fed army continued to capture horses whenever and wherever they could find them. On the streets of Nashville there were wagons and carriages sitting abandoned because the army had commandeered the horses. At Belle Meade plantation, Confederates from Hood's army took horses and supplies. At the telegraph office a message arrived from General Grant ordering Thomas to attack but the ice-covered city made it impossible to move. The cold was so bitter and biting that soldiers could only try to stay warm.

At a spring house some Union and Rebel soldiers met, exchanged newspapers, cigars and tobacco and chatted. My room at the St. Cloud was busy as people kept coming, telling me what they saw and heard and I wrote it all down as best I could.

CHAPTER 89

On Friday the ninth an ice storm hit Nashville full force around two in the afternoon. The cold paralyzed all activity and snow fell heavily. Men in the field stoked fires and sat beside them to stay warm. The only activity was gathering more wood for fires. However, as cold as it was in the soldier's camps, the theatres and circus in Nashville continued their shows.

It was just too cold to do anything that day; nobody could stand being outdoors unless they had no other choice. The Union Generals were huddled together in their headquarters and we heard that telegrams were coming from Washington, pushing them to fight, but nobody could fight in those conditions.

As cold as it was on the tenth, the next day was even colder. People skated on ponds and the ground was one huge sheet of ice. The police had it easy that day; criminals couldn't even get out and cause trouble. Ladies were ordered not to visit the front line. More sleet fell and winds blew across the city at around 60 miles an hour. The Rebel army was camped in the cold and most didn't have a cap for their head, shoes, blankets or tents. They were in an open field with no windbreaks, not much wood and thinly clad. The best they could do was sit as close to the fire as possible and try to stay warm.

The fires they built were in holes several feet deep in the ground. A fireplace was constructed on one side of the hole and a barrel chimney was made so that three sides had seats and beds. Wood ran out so the men gathered twigs and weeds to burn. There were weeds and rushes laid at the bottom of the pits, then blankets laid on top of that and men managed to keep warm that way. It was cold enough to kill a man but the Rebels survived because they built those little shelters that kept them from freezing.

At Traveller's Rest General Hood and the other Confederate Generals enjoyed a big, hot dinner.

On the twelfth the streets of Nashville were full of cavalry and wagons getting into place to attack the Rebel army. On the morning of December 13, the temperature was 13 degrees. Many of the Rebel soldiers were barefoot and starving. Soldiers from each army did reconnaissance and cannons were fired, but it was mostly quiet on the front lines. The big question was whether Hood would fight or pull out. There were Union bodies—dead and frozen hard as rock—too close to the Rebel lines to recover. Some of those were colored soldiers.

On the morning of the fourteenth the ground was still covered with ice and cannons were frozen to the ground. Now and then rifle fire erupted and a cannon sounded. The weather warmed as the day progressed and the sun melted some of the ice. It looked like there was a break in the weather.

The quick change in temperature brought fog and most of the city was covered in a mist, at one point so thick that it was impossible to see six feet in front of you. Everyone knew the Feds would attack but that did not stop Union soldiers from visiting Smokey Row; a fight there saw one soldier killed and another wounded.

CHAPTER 90

Well before sun-up on the morning of Thursday, December 15, bugles woke up Union soldiers. The fog was so thick that men could barely see in their own camps. Just before sunrise, bands played and music filled the air and Union soldiers moved to the front lines. There were still patches of snow and ice on the ground, but as the sun rose, the frozen ground turned to mud.

At four in the morning General Thomas, who stayed at the St. Cloud Hotel, left and rode into the fog and up Lawrence Hill, located just off Granny White Pike. Hood spent the night in the Overton home. Newspapers reported the Union army captured 30 Southern flags at the battle in Franklin and rumblings had started about Hood's judgment on his frontal assault against the Federal army and the casualties that resulted.

By nine the fog had cleared and the Union army advanced against the Rebels. All around the city cannons boomed—the first came from Fort Negley—and thunder rolled over the city. People in Gallatin and Lebanon heard the sound of cannons whose balls and shells cut down trees.

It was too foggy to attack early that morning so it was not until three hours later that actual fighting started, led by colored infantry.

There was heavy fighting all day on the fifteenth and Union forces clearly won the day. By six that evening both armies looked disorganized. The Confederate army under General Hood was outnumbered and fought valiantly but had to move backwards during the fighting so by the end of the day part of the army was at the intersection of Old Hickory Boulevard and Hillsboro Road. General Hood moved his headquarters from Traveller's Rest to the home of Judge John Lea, east of Granny White Pike.

Nashvillians came out and stood on hills to watch the battle but, although they rooted for the Rebs, their cheers were silent because the Feds had orders to put anyone to work who showed up at the front lines.

During that first afternoon, Mark Cockrill—75 years old—rode his horse into the battle, cheering on the Rebs. It was a miracle that no bullet or shell touched him. Over at Belle Meade, Miss Selene Harding, daughter of owner William Harding, stood on the front steps of their mansion waving her handkerchief and cheering on the Rebel army. There were bullets and shells falling all around her, but she refused to take shelter inside the house. She was an inspiration to the Reb soldiers that day.

By sunset—which was around 4:30 in the afternoon—soldiers were worn out from fighting.

General Hood was game to fight again the next day and organized his army in a line between Franklin Pike, across Granny White Pike, to Hillsboro Pike. The stone wall on Judge Lea's property was their cover.

It's hard to believe but the battle did not stop the evening's entertainment in downtown Nashville. The evening after the first battle, the Howes and Norton Circus played before a large audience while the play "Aladdin" was performed before an overflow crowd at the Old Temple and "Nalad Queen" played at the New Theatre.

It was business as usual on Smokey Row, too, as prostitutes plied their trade. It seems astounding but while soldiers fought and died on the battle field, many Nashville citizens enjoyed entertainment and diversions and business as usual. The Battle of Nashville did not change the daily lives of many of those who lived in Nashville.

After that first day, there were hospitals set up for wounded soldiers. On the east side of Franklin Pike, the beautiful mansion Glen Leven served as a hospital.

General Forrest was not in Nashville during the battle, although the Rebs desperately needed him. Instead, he was about 30 miles away in Murfreesboro, waiting for orders from General Hood to join the battle but those orders never came.

During the night Reb soldiers dug earthworks and prepared for another day of fighting. The Rebs were about a mile and a half further south than they were on the first day of battle and the soldiers were perplexed about Hood's motives when he sent his wagons south to Franklin, although Hood had no plans to fall back or retreat.

It was a busy, sleepless night for both sides with cannons firing and Rebs digging. In the Federal's camps, soldiers slept with their guns while Union cannons fired rounds into the Confederates.

CHAPTER 91

Before daybreak on Friday, December 16, Rebel soldiers were positioned on Overton Hill—also known as Peach Orchard Hill—and crossed the Franklin and Granny White Pikes over to Hillsboro Pike. The six mile long Confederate line of the day before had shrunk to three miles.

The temperature climbed into the 60s as the sun rose in the sky. On Peach Orchard Hill, General Stephen Lee's divisions served as the anchor for the right wing of the Rebs. None of those troops fought in the Battle of Franklin and hadn't seen much action the day before. Peach Orchard is a high hill and steep; except for a few trees and underbrush, it was mostly clear. A little after sun-up, colored troops in the Fed army attacked that hill, slipping and sliding on the muddy ground and took heavy losses. The Yankees attacked from the north and east, the steepest sides of that hill, with little cover, which meant Rebel defenders were in a strong position to defend that hill.

It was a noisy day; Fed cannons bellowed all day long while Reb cannons answered now and then as they portioned out their ammunition. The Yanks couldn't use their cannons much to help the colored troops because the lines of battle were so close. If they fired, they were liable to hit their own men.

As the Union soldiers got closer to the Rebs, there were barriers erected on Peach Orchard Hill they had to climb over and the Rebs poured on the fire. That didn't slow down the colored troops going up that hill; they let out their own Rebel yell and came at those Rebs, bound and determined to take the day. The Rebs would not give in and showed no mercy towards the colored. Those colored soldiers kept coming until the ground was covered with corpses wearing blue uniforms.

You could have walked up Peach Orchard hill and never touched the ground—just stepped on body after body—until you got to the top. There might have been 2,000 blue coats there—either killed or wounded—and there came a changing of the mind. Nobody on that hill doubted Negro soldiers would fight after that. The Rebs thought they would turn tail and run or were just too dumb to be a soldier, but that day the colored soldiers proved themselves. The problem the Feds faced was that, although the colored soldiers were brave and fought well, the Rebs still held Peach Orchard Hill.

The day kept getting warmer, a mist hung over the field and it began to rain. The left end of the Confederate line was anchored on Compton's Hill, just short of Hillsboro Pike, and Union cannons fired on them one after the other. Rebel sharpshooters did a good job of holding off Union soldiers but it was difficult to re-load because there was no break in the cannons firing.

The Rebels set up their defense at the highest point of Compton's Hill so they couldn't see Fed forces coming up the hill. It was a tactical error; if they had set up further down the hill they would have had a better view of Fed soldiers climbing toward them.

CHAPTER 92

By four o'clock the sky was dark and it was raining. There was a mist and the ground was thick with mud. The Rebs held Peach Orchard Hill for most of the day but around four the blue coated infantry came on strong and Reb soldiers panicked. At that point General Lee rode into the middle of those running Rebs, grabbed the colors and yelled "Rally, men, rally! For God's sake, rally! This is the place for brave men to die!"

Somebody said later that he looked like a God of War on his horse. He was a great leader, a man who inspired those panicked troops as he made himself a target for Union rifles.

In a quest for glory—and oh how those officers loved that Glory, no matter how many men had to die for them to get it—the Feds attacked Peach Orchard Hill. By this time, General Lee knew the Confederate army was beaten so they began pulling back as quickly as they could as the Feds mounted their charge up that hill.

The Rebel soldiers gathered themselves together so it wasn't a rout and moved back across Franklin Pike. General Cheatham had given orders that if a retreat was necessary it should be down Granny White Pike but the repeating rifles of the Feds forced the Rebs to move eastward from Granny White, over toward Franklin Pike.

The Feds decided to charge against the Reb lines on Compton's Hill and Governor Johnson came out to watch. It was getting dark fast that Friday and the Feds thought they would lose this battle and this day if they didn't hurry up and charge. A "decisive assault" they called it. They didn't want to have to fight the Rebs again the next day.

Compton's Hill is steep and there are places where it feels like you're going straight up. The Rebs were on top of that hill and about 4:15 that afternoon the Feds charged. There were Yanks pulling themselves up by vines and saplings and it didn't look very orderly but the Feds kept coming. The fact that the hill was so steep actually helped the blue bellies because the Rebs couldn't turn their cannons on them; they would have had to fire straight down and Reb infantry was dug in too far back from where they should have been to fire on the Yankees coming and when they tried they tended to overshoot the soldiers.

By the time the Yankees got to the top the Rebs realized they were outnumbered two or three to one so some Rebs fled while others stood their ground. The Rebs that stayed put up a good fight—they fought hand to hand with those blue coats while others tried to use their bayonets. Some of the artillery boys were swinging their swab sticks until the Feds overpowered them and demanded they surrender. Most of them did and when they did the blue coats shot them.

Lieutenant Colonel William Shy refused to give up and fought like the devil until a Union officer, only three or four feet away, shot him in the head. They took Shy to Felix Compton's house where he died and later that hill was renamed Shy's Hill.

The Union flag was planted on top of Shy's Hill and then the Feds took the Reb's cannon and turned it on them as the Rebs headed South. They weren't going to stop until they got to Corinth.

It was just chaos and confusion as night came on with bodies—black and white—scattered all over the ground, twisted, turned, laying on each other, some piled on each other five deep. Nobody knew who was dead and people were scared to learn.

Around ten o'clock that night the Rebs were on Franklin Pike or in the dark woods. It made you sick to see those Rebel soldiers running the other way. There was no hope left, no hope whatsoever. It was over and done and nobody was looking for the Rebs to come back and lick those Yanks. If they had come back, they'd a been licked again.

The blue bellies kept chasing and it seemed like there was no end to the number of Fed soldiers pursuing. Now and then some Rebel soldiers turned and fired their rifles at the blue wave but mostly the Rebs just kept running south.

Those Yank soldiers were so close that Johnny Reb could see faces and when they saw that a lot of those Yanks had black faces it made them madder and madder. They were running from Negroes and, for a Southern white soldier, there couldn't be anything more humiliating than that.

The Rebs put up a barrier across Granny White Pike down around Brentwood so the Feds couldn't run them down if they chased. At the barricade a Rebel cavalry made a stand in the rain against Union troops and General Hood ordered the Rebs to hold that position until the Rebel army escaped. The Union troops charged and the fighting was fierce but the Rebs held their ground in those hills, falling back a little at a time in spite of odds against them. Those barricades held the Feds up for several hours, by which time the Rebs were a lot further south. Finally, around midnight in the rain the Rebels got to Old Hickory just as snow started to mix with rain.

CHAPTER 93

A lot of Rebel soldiers were captured but those Rebs didn't want to surrender to a colored man. There was one case where a white officer told a black soldier to find a white man cause he wasn't gonna surrender to no nigger. Well, that Reb officer changed his mind when he heard the click of that Negro's rifle.

The Rebels felt no honor surrendering to a Negro, especially officers cause those Negroes might have been their slaves just a few short years back. One Reb Captain grabbed a gun from a guard and shot a Negro and as soon as he did a white Fed officer ran a sword through him.

If a colored soldier or an officer commanding colored soldiers surrendered to Rebs, they were in for some bad treatment. There were three white officers who led colored troops who were caught, stripped and made to march for almost two days stark naked. Finally, the Rebs led them to a ravine and shot all three in the head.

Those blue coats could be stupid mean. A Reb soldier, Thomas Benton Smith, surrendered, gave up his gun and was led off when an officer struck him in the head with his saber—hit him hard and kept hitting him until there were deep gashes in his head. His skull laid open, his brain was exposed and nobody expected him to live—but he did. That was a miracle but he was never right after that. His brain was addled and his mind was gone.

Almost every single church was a hospital that night and there were wounded soldiers in private homes and public buildings. If the army found a horse and carriage they turned them into an ambulance. At the Felix Compton home there were about 150 soldiers—blue and grey—laying there.

All day Saturday the wounded and dead were brought into the city. There were a couple thousand casualties from that battle and they were joined by those wounded at the Battle of Franklin. The Reb prisoners were put on a train to Louisville and on that first train over 300 Confederate officers were sent North.

On Monday the nineteenth, General Forrest came to Hood's headquarters before sunup. Hood wanted to stay in Tennessee but General Forrest pumped some sense into his head. He told Hood in no uncertain terms that he and what was left of his army needed to keep moving South past the Tennessee River. General Hood finally saw the light and General Forrest and his troops, with some help from other troops, covered the Reb's rear as they headed south.

Retreat means defeat and there isn't much honor in an army that's been defeated. The soldiers were exhausted—mentally, physically and emotionally—from the battles they had fought. The grey coats left everything when they ran—guns, food, ammunition, wagons—and now they had to hang their head in shame and keep marching, whether they had shoes or not. The sad fact is that many of those Reb soldiers had to march barefooted all the way down into Mississippi.

To top it off there was a snowstorm with heavy sleet as the Rebs headed South and the only thing they had to eat was a piece of half-baked bread to go along with that miserable weather. As they trudged South the realization hit each man, one by one, that not only had they lost a battle—actually, two big battles in the last three weeks—but the Confederacy was lost. The idea of free blacks rankled them, but they had to face that slavery was done and over and many concluded that without slavery the South was no longer equal to the North. A hatred of Union soldiers burned inside the heart of many Rebel soldiers.

CHAPTER 94

It was closing in on Christmas as the Southern army marched south. In Nashville, the Union occupiers relaxed some of their rules and allowed Nashville citizens to take Reb prisoners food and gifts. An intense feeling of humiliation was embedded deeply in the Nashville citizens who supported the Southern cause and many prisoners of War agreed to take the Amnesty Oath so they could go home.

On Christmas Eve there was four inches of snow on the ground as the Southern army continued moving toward the Tennessee River. On Christmas Day, the Rebels began crossing that river near Florence, Alabama.

In Nashville there was a parade downtown by the Masons two days after Christmas and cannons boomed to celebrate Sherman's capture of Savannah; Nashvillians had just received that news.

The Yanks quit chasing the Rebs at the Tennessee River but the grey army kept going until they arrived in Tupelo, Mississippi.

On New Year's Eve Billy came to my room and handed me a letter; it was from General Forrest. It read, "Dear Mr. Duncan, I regret to inform you that your son, Edward, lost his life on Christmas Day while defending our soldiers against Federal forces in pursuit. Edward was an excellent soldier, brave in battle and courageous in his actions. He was a valuable member of my force and it is with a heavy heart that I must inform you of his death." It was signed, "Your obedient servant, Gnl N.B Forrest."

I put down the letter and was choked with sobs. I sat in my room, the letter in my hand, for several hours, numb with disbelief. I had lost two sons in this terrible War. I did not read that letter again but the words were burned into my mind. I knew every word by heart and they repeated themselves to me over and over as I sat in my chair. It was after daybreak before I got up from that chair.

I saw Mrs. Monahan and Rachel at breakfast that morning and they looked down at their plates when they saw me. I passed them by and sat at another table. I saw that Rachel's eyes were red and swollen.

CHAPTER 95

The winter of 1864-1865 was colder than usual—bitter cold—and the Rebel army under General Hood, or what was left of it, was in Tupelo, Mississippi. There were, at most, about 15,000 infantry. There was very little food and few blankets to keep them warm. General Hood requested to be relieved of his command and the Confederate government in Richmond put Lieutenant General Richard Taylor in temporary command. People said of Hood that he was "an excellent soldier but a poor general" and that about sums it up, as far as I can see.

In January, the Army of Tennessee ceased to exist and a few thousand of the soldiers headed east to the Carolinas where they planned to reinforce General Joe Johnston's army as he attempted to stop Sherman, marching north towards Grant in Virginia.

In Nashville, wooden markers that had been placed on graves disappeared, taken by those needing fire wood. The city had grown; the population of 30,000 when the Fed army came down the Cumberland River in February, 1862 had swelled to 75,000, not counting Union soldiers in town.

On January 9, a Constitutional Convention was held at the Capitol in Nashville in order get the government back in the hands of the people. Trouble was, the Unionists—and this convention was organized by Unionists—knew that if there was a free, open election, the Rebels would be back in power the day after.

The convention added two amendments to the State Constitution. The first one wiped out the act from 1861 that put Tennessee in the Confederacy and the second abolished slavery in the state. However, even though all slaves were declared free, the convention would not allow Negroes to vote. The convention then nominated Parson Brownlow for Governor.

On February 22—President George Washington's Birthday—there was a state-wide vote to ratify the Amendments to the Constitution and only three voted against it. There was a one hundred gun salute at the Capitol. That same day news came that Charleston had fallen.

On February 24, Governor Johnson left for Washington to be sworn in as Vice President. We were glad to get rid of him but wondered how much further damage he could do as a member of the Federal government. Of course, a Vice President really has no power or influence; he's just a buzzard sitting on the shoulder of the President. As long as Abe Lincoln was President, Andrew Johnson was just another politician strutting his stuff without doing much harm.

The government let Confederate deserters return home in January if they took the Amnesty Oath and announced they intended to be law abiding citizens. President Andrew Jackson's nephew and private secretary, Andrew Jackson Donelson, came back to Nashville and took the Amnesty Oath and so did John Overton, although the authorities were pretty skeptical of Overton. The Big Boys in Nashville figured that Overton had finally realized the Confederacy was whipped and he might lose Traveller's Rest. Overton had been with the Confederate army before the Feds took over Nashville and was a Southern patriot through and through. The acting Provost

Marshal informed Overton that what he did during the War was treason as Overton settled in at Traveller's Rest.

The guerrillas had not given up; there was still much activity around Nashville. A wood train was attacked about six miles south of Nashville and a Tennessee and Alabama passenger train was captured at Spring Hill and railroad track on the Louisville and Nashville line was ripped up just south of Bowling Green. About seven miles west of Nashville a train of wagons on Harding Pike was attacked and an L&N freight train was derailed—an engine and five cars went down an embankment—just north of Mitchellville.

CHAPTER 96

On March 4, Parson Brownlow was elected Governor of Tennessee as well as an entire Union slate of lawmakers. Few turned out to vote because they wouldn't allow anyone who opposed them to run. The election meant a hundred guns were fired at the state Capitol. That same day Abraham Lincoln was sworn in for his second term as President and Andrew Johnson was sworn in as Vice President. We got word that ole Andy was pretty drunk when it came time to give his speech.

On March 20 the streets of Nashville were filled with Negroes who paraded through the city singing and praying. They were celebrating the end of slavery in Tennessee and wanted to elevate themselves, they said, so there was a banner that said "We can forgive and forget the wrongs of the past." The Negroes seemed sincere in wanting to forget about their slave past and move on, be good Christians and become an educated people.

The old, submissive Negro was a relic of the past. This change did not set well with most of the white citizens of Nashville. They called the Negroes "deadheads" and characterized them as "lazy," "insolent" and "depraved." They did not feel the Negro was capable of surviving on his own and wondered what their own reaction would be when those Negroes came crawling back, begging to be taken care of and sheltered. There would be some payback, of course, some settling of the score, but for now, it was just uncomfortable to see Negroes not in their place, acting like they were as good as white folks. "There'll come a day, yessir, there'll come a day," the white folks kept saying, "and when that day comes, we'll be here, just a-waitin'."

On April third came news that Richmond had fallen, which caused another hundred guns to go off at the Capitol. Business stopped in Nashville and newsboys had a field day selling newspapers that told of a Union Victory. The next day Parson Brownlow was certified as Governor by the legislature. He was the only candidate to run, so his victory wasn't a mystery but the election, as one sided as it was, ended military government in Nashville. The 13th Amendment to the Federal Constitution, which abolished slavery in the United States, was ratified by the legislature that same day.

On April 10 we received word that General Lee had surrendered to General Grant in Virginia. The news of the surrender was posted on the bulletin board outside the Dispatch's office on Deaderick Street around nine in the morning and it wasn't long before the news was all over town. I'd never seen a crowd gather as fast as the one that formed in front of the newspaper's office, hungry for more news. Copies of the newspaper sold out quickly.

There seemed to be more relief than disappointment in that news. The fighting had gone on for so long and taken a toll on everyone, from the boys in the army to wives and mothers at home, farmers and planters whose crops and livestock had been taken and all those who lost their homes, their land, and loved ones. When news of the surrender was announced at the Capitol, both houses of the legislature celebrated and then adjourned. There were cannons booming and guns firing while at the Maxwell Barracks the soldiers cheered so loud you couldn't hear yourself think.

Saturday, April 15, was proclaimed a day of thanksgiving and rejoicing by Mayor Smith.

CHAPTER 97

On Saturday, April 15 the ceremonies were set to start at ten in the morning to celebrate the end of the War. Businesses were closed and a parade of about 15,000 soldiers, led by several Union Generals along with several military bands, was set to march from Fort Negley to the Public Square. The celebrations were scheduled to last all day and into the night; that evening there would be fireworks and bands would play.

There were flags, signs and decorations on most of the buildings in Nashville. It looked like it was going to be a great day for a celebration; the sky was clear at sunrise but then dark clouds rolled in and it looked like it might rain. Still, it seemed like almost everyone in Nashville was in a festive mood and ready to join in a celebration.

Then the telegraph office received the message that President Lincoln had been assassinated. There was a numbness of disbelief as people wondered if it could be true and were certain that it was at the same time. There was checking and rechecking of the news and it was confirmed over and over.

It became real quiet as the news sunk in. Nobody said a word, and then a huge sorrow descended, like a dark cloud, over the crowd, and tears and hurt broke out. Some of the Unionists thought of punishing Confederate sympathizers for Lincoln's death but those feelings were held in check. Instead, a feeling of distress, of deep in the gut sorrow, took hold and a hollow disbelief that could not find words to adequately express feelings and thoughts invaded our souls. Never in our history had a President been assassinated and it stunned everyone who heard the news. Even most Southern loyalists could not fathom such an event and felt a loss.

The authorities ordered the Union soldiers to go back to their barracks and bands played funeral dirges as tears ran down faces of brave men and women. Flags were lowered to half mast and the dry goods store opened so people could purchase black crepe to hang on their houses and other buildings.

Deep grief renders the body helpless, numbs the soul, makes the heart heavy and buries the spirit under a weight so crushing that it cannot rise. To be in such a celebratory mood and then plunge into a grief like that is hard on the heart. It's almost like the heart stops beating.

The rest of that day guns were fired and people wanted more news so the newspapers kept printing extra editions. The biggest shock came when it was learned that an actor who had performed at the Nashville Theatre in early 1864—John Wilkes Booth—was the man who shot the President.

A few die-hard Rebs laughed and cheered at the death of the President and some of those were shot or bayoneted right on the spot. Those who could not hide their Southern loyalties hid away that day. Not many were even thinking of Andrew Johnson, but he was now President of the United States.

President Lincoln's funeral was on Wednesday, April 19, and businesses in Nashville were closed while the city was in mourning. There was a funeral procession beginning at ten that morning at Fort Negley which went to the Public Square. Bands played dirges and a catafalque covered in black cloth drawn by twelve horses—six white and six black—followed by Union soldiers and officers, then city officers—Judges, the Mayor, City Council, and the fire department. The freed Negroes came last.

Out beside Harding Pike was a field where a speaker's platform stood but a thunder storm, with sharp lightning and heavy thunder, dampened the crowd. A Union General and Governor Brownlow spoke that day, which was the most somber day I'd ever experienced.

That entire day felt heavy and slow. It was a day when you could not smile or feel joy; people moved with no quickness or lightness. I felt an almost religious awakening as I realized that nobody—no matter how important and essential—was really necessary. Men will come and go but the world will go on; it will continue turning and new life will continue being born. It was a somber revelation and certainly not earth shattering, but it changed me forever.

CHAPTER 98

The War was over. The Army of Tennessee surrendered in North Carolina at the end of April, and in May, General Thomas reviewed a field filled with Union troops south of downtown. Somebody said there were 20,000 troops there.

General Thomas announced that the surrender of guerrillas would be accepted on the same terms extended to Generals Lee and Johnston. In May, Ellis Harper brought 24 men in to Gallatin and they were paroled. That group operated in northern Sumner and Robertson counties. Duval McNairy reported in Franklin and was paroled; he operated in the Franklin area during the War. Champ Ferguson was not pardoned; he admitted to killing 33 people and the Provost Marshal decided his crimes were too awful to be excused.

President Johnson pardoned the Rebels and gave them amnesty unless they were still rich. The state of Tennessee got its archives and assets back at the end of May when three former members of Governor Isham Harris' administration came to Nashville with about $600,000 and the state's files. There was a reward of $5,000 on Governor Harris' head; nobody knew where he was.

There were no jobs for the Negroes and there were shortages of food and shelter but during the summer there were a number of schools established, mostly by Northern philanthropic societies, to help the Negro. In June, General Clinton Fisk arrived in Nashville, determined to educate former slaves.

The slaves had food, clothing and shelter supplied to them by their masters before the War; during the War the Union army took care of them but when the War ended they were on their own and it was a struggle to survive.

In early June, a Union officer came up to me while I was dining at the St. Cloud and handed me a sheet of paper. "You need to sign this," he said.

It was a long piece of paper, an "Amnesty Proclamation," issued by President Andrew Johnson. It stated, "I hereby grant to all persons who have, directly or indirectly, participated in the existing rebellion, except as hereinafter excepted, amnesty and pardon, with restoration of all rights of property, except as to slaves, and except in cases where legal preceedings, under the laws of the United States."

The sheet read "I" and then there was a blank for my name, "do solemnly swear, in presence of Almighty God, that I will henceforth faithfully support, protect, and defend the Constitution of the United States, and the union of the States thereunder, and that I will, in like manner, abide by, and faithfully support all laws and proclamations which have been made during the existing rebellion with reference to the emancipation of slaves. So help me God."

I signed it.

CHAPTER 99

It had been a difficult year in Nashville; the city still had Union troops and bad blood was headed towards a boil with the administration of Governor Parson Brownlow, who was determined to exact revenge on those who sided with the Confederacy during the War. He intended to punish the former Rebels and set about doing it by keeping former Confederates out of government offices. He drove through the Constitutional Amendment abolishing slavery and the Amendment to give blacks the right to vote. Tennessee was one of the first states to do so and his actions led Tennessee to re-join the Union in 1866.

Parson Brownlow was the most hated man in Tennessee. Some called him the worst governor of all time and there is no doubt in my mind that his actions as Governor played a major role in the formation of the Ku Klux Klan.

On the last day of June, Rachel's mother, Mrs. Monahan died; Rachel continued to live at the St. Cloud. I expected her to find a young man to marry, but she confessed that she could not find any young man suitable for marriage. There were few young men to choose from; the War had taken the lives of so many and those who returned were haunted by the specter of battles and bodies laying wounded or dead in fields. Still, she certainly had young men who called on her, wishing to court her, but she turned them all away.

I confessed that I thought she and Edward might marry after the War but she surprised me when she said "I never thought of Edward as a husband." She was an independent woman and could ignore what others thought; there were Union officers and soldiers who remained in Nashville after the War but she said she would rather die an old maid than marry someone who had fought against the Confederate army.

One day she surprised me with a letter from Matthew. I had not seen him since the surrender and, although he had worked for the Union side, I hoped we might reconcile. I was certainly ready to forgive and forget; I loved my son—who was now my only son—and wanted to seek him out.

Rachel said she had seen Matthew several days earlier and he wanted me to have a letter, but not for three days. She kept that promise and apologized as she handed me his letter, which read, "Dear Father, I have decided to venture West. This has been a difficult time and I hope I can make a new start. I hear there is opportunity in the West and I want to seek my fortune there. Please know that throughout this ordeal I have loved you and will continue to do so. Your loving son, Matthew."

I put the letter in my lap and, once again, felt a heaviness in my heart and soul. I had not lost just two sons in this War; I had lost all three and felt heavy-hearted and terribly alone. I never heard from Matthew again.

In the Fall of 1865 I was 53 years old; there was a 27 year difference between me and Rachel and I saw that difference as insurmountable for the true happiness of two people but she disagreed and confessed she had always had a deep fondness for me.

On Christmas Day, 1865, Rachel and I were married. I never thought I would marry again; I had loved my wife, Mary and we shared a good life together. I felt I had grown to an old age and did not have many years left on this earth. I was wrong; I have lived 25 years past the beginning of that War and am still active and healthy. I am now 90 and Rachel is 63 so what was once an unmatched couple, an old man and a young woman, is now an old couple.

Rachel and I have four children; the oldest is 25 and the youngest is 18, two girls and two boys, and they are the pride and joy of our lives. Mary and I had three children who lived past childhood and I expected to end my days on Earth with progeny until this War was thrust upon us. But God has His own plans and now my two sons and two daughters with Rachel will carry the line of "Duncan" into the future as all four children will, I expect, bear our descendents. We now have four grandchildren; I never thought I would ever know that blessing.

Rachel and I have lived in Nashville since the War ended but I could not stay retired; instead, I went back to work, first with newspapers and then as a businessman. It has been a good life and I am thankful to have lived this long in good health all these years.

I began writing down these memories and history on January 1, 1890 because I felt this story needed to be told. During the past 12 years I continued to add to it from time to time. I have written honestly but I have not revealed all I know because some of those who lived during the War years are still alive and do not want others to know of all they did during those years. There were poor, obscure men who were brave and wealthy, prominent men who were cowards. I have found the prominent and wealthy often compromised the principles they proclaimed when it threatened their wealth and position. The poor man had nothing to lose in terms of wealth and power so he often stood alone. That was not always the case with either the wealthy or the poor, but it was the case for some of those still living in this community.

War is a madness that seizes our hearts and tells us that we will be brave, that War will bring us glory and honor and make us heroes. War is a madness that seizes our minds and chases away reason; it is a madness that captures our soul and challenges our belief in God. Most of all, War is a madness to which we succumb from time to time, especially if a generation has not known War. New generations often see War as a way to define themselves.

I did not fire a single shot in the War now commonly referred to as the Civil War and I did not participate in a single battle but I, too, was wounded in that War and part of me died back then. I am still haunted by memories, by decisions, by young men who are not alive today because of that War. I know of countless mothers who lost sons and whose lives have been lived with a gaping hole where the love for a child should reside. I know fathers whose faces show no emotion but whose souls are wracked by the loss of a son—or sons—who will not carry forth their name. I know of women who never married because their true love died on a battlefield. I know other women whose lives have been spent caring for a man whose wounds never allowed him to work enough to support his family and whose pain is also carried by his loved ones.

There is always an end to a War but War never ends for those who do the fighting. Those who fight in a War and survive carry with them haunted dreams, disturbing memories and an ongoing disbelief because they can never explain how or why they survived while others did not. For those who fought in battles where cannons boomed and bullets flew, there is no restful sleep, there is no day when part of their mind is not remembering. There is no heart that is undivided, there is no soul that does not ache. Those who fought in Wars have no words to describe battles in a way that communicates every thought, feeling and impulse that courses through a mind and body as he faces death.

There are those amongst us who look back after all these years and are thankful to be alive, amazed they are alive and who have lulled themselves into remembering War as a grand and glorious adventure. These are men whose souls are washed in forgiveness for what they did and what was done to them, but that forgiveness does not come with forgetting; that is a price too big to ever be paid. The men today who look back at War tend to feed the romantic spirit in young men who long to show bravery and win glory on the field of battle and that is why War will never end. That is why young men always yearn for a War to prove their manhood, to show the world there are things worth fighting for so they are willing to fight. But all who fight in Wars come to realize that so much of War is brutal, barbaric and unnecessary, that wounds leave scars that never heal and memories may be buried but are never erased.

I have known brave men and I have seen cowardice. I have heard stories of what men have done in battle and how they faced—or ran from—guns firing at them. I have heard tales of young men who refused to grow old by racing into a line of fire. I have felt the sorrow of mothers and fathers whose sons have fallen in battle and I have glimpsed the emptiness inside those who survived a War and I can say with certainty that there is a peace at the end of a War but War never ends in peace.

www.ingramcontent.com/pod-product-compliance
Lightning Source LLC
Chambersburg PA
CBHW020258030826
48979CB00026B/1391/J

* 9 7 8 0 9 8 5 5 5 6 1 2 9 *